RESISTING FATE

KYLIE GILMORE

Cover design by Sweet 'N Spicy Designs

Published by: Extra Fancy Books

ISBN-13: 978-1-942238-37-9

Because a romance book club would rock…

1

____

Don't smite me. Ben Wright quickly stepped through the entrance of St. Joseph's Catholic Church and lived to tell the tale. He hadn't set foot in church since he was a kid. He veered right and headed downstairs to the basement for the craft bazaar. Not that he was a crafty guy. He was more of a rugged type with his six-foot height, short light brown hair, and his usual black leather jacket with worn jeans and hiking boots. His dimpled smile detracted from the ruggedness, making him "approachable" or "such a cutie patootie," as Grandmom always said when she wanted to butter him up. Just like she'd said this morning before ordering him to pick up a jar of homemade cherry jam and a handknit sweater. Something in a men's large that he'd promptly forget he bought. *Merry Christmas to me!*

He chuckled to himself. Grandmom was down with a cold or flu, she wasn't sure, and had insisted he do exactly as she said. "It's one day only! You can't miss it!" And when he'd assured her he didn't need anything more than to spend Christmas with her, healthy and well, she'd become irritated, shooing him out the door with a parting jab. "You have to get your gift before someone else snatches it up!" Like there'd be a stampede for men's handknit sweaters.

In any case, he always came through for a woman in need. It was kind of his thing.

He halted in the bustling basement, surprised by the number of people Christmas shopping when it was still November. It sure as hell felt like Christmas down here, from the silver garland strung along the ceiling to the carols playing softly in the background to the scent of hot chocolate and fresh-baked goodies. He shoved his hands in his jeans pockets, taking in way too many long tables along the edges of the space bursting with crafty crap. He needed a plan—get in, get out.

He made his way to the center refreshment table with hot chocolate, juice boxes, and assorted individually wrapped baked goods for sale. He figured the women there could direct him to the jam. A few minutes later, jam in hand, he was about to ask where the men's sweaters were hiding when a hand clapped him on the shoulder.

"Ben, how nice to see you here again!"

He startled at the sight of an ancient Father Munson, completely bald now and considerably more cheerful than he'd ever been at Mass. Ben flushed, feeling guilty for…*every-thing*. "How're you, Father?"

"I'm well, thank you. Your grandmother said you'd be here. Let me direct you to the sweaters she thought you might like."

"Sure, thanks." He followed him through the crowd to the far corner of the room, where two long tables were covered in sheep's haircuts. One corner of his mouth lifted, imagining all those naked sheep grazing in the meadow.

Father Munson gestured him on. "Right over there," he said and took off, surprisingly nimble for a man of his years.

Ben stood near the end of one table next to a couple of elderly women checking out the men's sweaters. There were also hats, scarves, and mittens. He touched the edge of a hat, already feeling itchy and hot. Okay, as soon as those women moved on, he'd grab the first sweater close to his size and get out of here. But then his grandmother would want to see him wear it, and she'd notice if he only wore it once.

The women moved on, and he stepped forward, setting the jam on the table and quickly sifting through the men's sweaters for one large enough for his wide shoulders that wasn't too hideous. He felt someone staring at him. He lifted his head and nearly laughed. Her again? What were the odds?

Missy Higgins. Formerly red-haired, currently brunette with sharp brown eyes, delicate-looking cheekbones and nose, and the sexiest plump lips with a dip at the top. She wore a clingy red sweater that showed every sweet curve.

This was gonna be fun. The first time he'd met her months ago at his honorary brother Marcus's bar in the city, she'd caught his eye with her red hair. But then she'd dyed her gorgeous red hair dark brown, and the second time he met her, he hadn't recognized her. By the time he put it together, she was irritated. But not in a serious way, more like she didn't really give a fuck.

He slapped a palm on the table. "Missy Higgins, this must be fate!"

She shook her head, smiling and shifting to stand across from him. "Uh, sure. A magical force brought us to the church basement. How romantic."

Her deadpan delivery cracked him up. "You have to admit it was a magical force that had us going through the revolving door of Claire's hotel at the same time." That was where he'd met her when her hair was brown.

"Fate must work pretty slow. That was three weeks ago, and you didn't even remember me."

"I remembered you."

A small smile played over her lips. "No, you didn't."

"Well, you changed your hair. It was a delayed—"

She lifted a palm, cutting him off. "And it was perfectly logical that we went through the door at the same time. I was coming in for the jacket I forgot, and you were coming out to give it to me."

"Fate," he said ominously.

Her brown eyes lit with amusement. "Coincidence."

"And what about last week at the deli?"

She rolled her eyes. "We work in the same town. Bound to happen."

"But it never happened before." He lifted a finger. "Once is coincidence." He added another finger. "Twice is—"

"Random."

He bit back a smile. "Unusual." He held up three fingers. "And three times, well, even a hard-core nonbeliever like yourself has to admit is—" he went for a deep spooky voice "—fate."

"Oo-oo-oh," she said flatly, wiggling her fingers in the air. "Looking for a sweater?"

"Under grandmother's orders."

"Oh, the women's sweaters are down the other end. Cheryl can help you." She gestured to a woman at a second table full of knits.

"It's for me. I'm buying my own Christmas present."

She laughed out loud, a throaty soft roll of a laugh.

He lifted the jar of jam and gave her his approachable sexy charmer of a dimpled smile. "Got this too. Not sure if this is for me or for her."

Her lips curved in a small smile. "What a good grandson, doing her Christmas shopping."

He shrugged one shoulder. "She isn't feeling well, but she didn't want to miss out on all these fine knits. I'm her only grandkid. Obviously she spoils me."

"Obviously. Size?"

He set the jam down and threw his shoulders back. "Large enough for this manly chest."

"Uh-huh." Her eyes lit with amusement. "So we're looking for a petite?"

"*Extra* large," he drawled in a voice that implied more.

"Maybe a poncho, then?" she asked before pressing her lips together, clearly fighting back a laugh.

"Don't quit your day job. You're a terrible saleswoman."

She smiled cheekily and started going through the sweaters. "I'm sure there's something..." She pulled a dark green sweater out and held it up.

"There's a bird on it."

She glanced down at it. "It's the bluebird of happiness." She met his eyes with a straight face. "No?"

"No."

She lifted another sweater. "Reindeer? Great for Christmas day with granny." At his silence, she tried again. "Snowman. And look, there's even some tiny snowballs."

"Next," he growled.

She held up another sweater and made a face. "This one is kind of boring, but maybe that's your style."

Smart-ass. It was a plain dark gray, the least hideous in the bunch, but if he said he wanted that one, he risked sounding boring.

The greater risk—looking like a complete dork with a bird, reindeer, or snowman emblazoned on his chest—had him narrowing his eyes. "Is there even a question?" He reached for the plain gray sweater, and she shoved the bird sweater in his hand instead.

"I knew it," she said with a sly grin. "You're a bluebird of happiness kind of..." She trailed off, stiffening, the color draining from her face.

"Are you okay?"

"Su-sure." She swallowed visibly and met his eyes with a pinched expression. "Great."

"Then why're you as white as a communion wafer?"

His first Catholic joke fell flat. She regarded him gravely before leaning close and whispering, "Pretend you're my boyfriend."

He looked around. "Is there some guy—oh, hey." She was next to him, closer than she'd ever been, her head level with his chest, her scent floral and fresh. She grabbed his arm and pulled him back behind the table with her.

Before he had a chance to put an arm around her like the possessive boyfriend he never was, she was pressed up against his front, her fingers running through his hair, smiling at him like he was the only man in the room. And it worked. Hell yeah, it worked. He slipped his arms around her waist, keeping her close.

"Hello, gorgeous," he said, his voice rough with lust.

Her eyes widened for a moment before she cupped the back of his neck, drawing him down to whisper in his ear, "We've been together for a year. Serious."

He slid a hand into her hair, momentarily distracted by its silky softness; then he whispered near her ear, "Two months is my longest relationship. This must be fate."

"Ha-ha." She wrapped her arms around his neck and shifted them so his back was to the room. She peered around him.

"All clear?" he asked.

"Fuck." She shifted him again so they were sideways to the room.

"Okay." He rested his hands lightly on her waist. It was almost like slow dancing.

"Pretend we're talking." She gave him a tight smile, dropping one arm from him. Her other hand went back to playing with the hair at the nape of his neck.

He let go of her waist and lifted a hand, stroking one finger along her soft cheek. "Come here often?"

She focused fully on him, giving him a sexy smile, her voice husky. "Not often enough, sugar."

Holy pretend girlfriend, he was turned on.

He played with a lock of her hair, studying the silky strands. "Why did you dye your pretty red hair dark brown?"

"Because I hate it."

"I don't."

"Then you can dye your light brown hair pretty red."

He snorted. "Seriously, though, why do you hate it?"

Her hand on the back of his neck tightened as she looked out to the room.

"Missy—" Her lips met his suddenly, hot and sweet. The sights and sounds of a crafty Christmas wonderland faded as his hand came up to hold her jaw, deepening the kiss, electric heat surging through his veins. She tasted of peppermint and sin, and he couldn't get enough. He feasted on that luscious mouth like a starving man.

She tore her mouth away, breathless, eyes wide.

His heart beat in his ears, pulse thrumming. He stared at her pink lips, full and soft.

She met him halfway for a second kiss.

He didn't care that it was pretend because it felt so right. Then her tongue darted out to touch his, instinct took over, and he dove in for more.

2

—————

Missy stepped away from Ben, breathless and stunned by the intensity of the kiss they'd just shared. Her knees were actually weak, like she needed to sit down. So she did, pulling out the cushioned chair tucked close to the table. He remained standing, his large hand sliding under her hair, cupping her neck, warm and reassuring. She let herself enjoy his touch for a long moment while she collected herself before standing abruptly, dislodging his hand. The busy church basement came back into focus. She needed to know if Louis was still here.

Ben slipped an arm around her waist, distracting her with his sexy rumble in her ear. He smelled like warm spice and leather. "Who're we looking for? You want me to kick his ass?"

She clenched her jaw. Louis was her problem, and she dealt with her problems alone.

"Just a minute," she said under her breath. She went up on tiptoe, craning her neck for the tall, thin man with scraggly black hair, wearing an old army jacket. Her ex-husband was a drugged-out homeless man. She wouldn't have given a shit except he showed up at her apartment a couple of weeks ago demanding money, probably for his next score. She suppressed a shudder. He'd been stalking her ever since, saying she owed him. She knew to keep an eye out for an old blue Toyota Camry that he lived in and probably stole. Even if she had money, she'd never give him a cent. Her hatred for him had faded over the last nine years, but she'd never, ever forgive him.

He seemed to be gone. She let out a breath and sank to the chair. Louis must be desperate to look her up after so many years. Maybe he owed money to a drug lord, or maybe he just needed his next hit of whatever he was on. She didn't care what he did as long as he moved on. Eventually he would give up on her and move on to richer pastures. She was sure he must have a list of exes to hit up for cash. He used to be smooth with women and handsome when he cleaned up.

She glanced up at Ben still standing by her side—the perfect shield to scare off another man. At first glance, Ben looked tough with his short-cropped hair, angular face with pronounced cheekbones and a square jaw with a hint of stubble. Plus he was tall and built, the black leather jacket emphasizing his wide shoulders and broad chest. She knew he was harmless and not just because he clearly adored his grandmother. She'd put Ben in the harmless category the first time they met months ago at a party. They'd played as a team at pool, where he'd been a charming flirt, and they'd trounced the competition. That was the kind of victory she remembered. When he later didn't remember her, she was less than flattered, but it just confirmed that his flirting had no serious intent behind it. Harmless.

Except that kiss—not so harmless. It was lethal, stealing her breath, clouding her mind, reducing her to a quivery needy state. A flirt she could handle, anything stronger than that might lead to relationship land, a place she swore never to visit again. The fact that her marriage of three years had turned abusive would have been reason enough. But she was a *survivor*, determined to feel comfortable around men again and hold her own. Years of therapy and self-defense classes got her to where she was today—single and safe, dealing with men on her own casual terms.

No man was trustworthy.

She knew this from Louis, from her years volunteering at a women's shelter in Seattle, and her current volunteer work for a women's emergency hotline. Even knowing all that, she'd let her guard down last spring, getting involved with a short-term employee at the construction firm where she worked. She'd agreed with her boyfriend, Matt, to keep it quiet so it wouldn't look like she, the person in charge of payroll among many other things, had a special attachment to an employee. Matt would be leaving in the summer as soon as the project ended, so she hadn't thought it was a big deal. She'd spent many nights in his studio apartment, furnished sparsely with a mattress on the floor and a sofa. She didn't care that he didn't have money because he was so warm and affectionate. He'd actually made her feel cherished, something she'd never felt before with any man. When his temp job ended three months later, she'd been so excited to finally tell the world about their relationship, and then Matt informed her they couldn't go public because he was married with a baby on the way. Total betrayal.

Missy was so humiliated, so embarrassed, she'd never told a soul about it. Lesson learned once again—this time for keeps—no man was trustworthy. She had her sister, her friends, and that was more than enough.

She looked up at Ben, defenses firmly in place. He pushed her hair back over her ear, gazing down at her with heat in his blue eyes. She felt herself flush. Normally she wouldn't be opposed to acting on fantastic chemistry for a hookup, but Ben was one of the guys who'd grown up close to the Campbell family. And the Campbell clan, with all their biological and honorary brothers, were frequently at the bar where Missy and her friends from book club hung out. Some of the guys had recently become engaged or married to some of her friends, and the crossover between the two groups had reached epic proportions. She was sure to run into Ben more and more frequently. The fact that she'd only seen him a handful of times before this was not enough to sway her. She liked to keep her casual hookups separate from her real life.

She stood, embarrassingly overheated from their kiss. "Thanks for your help."

He jerked his chin. "Who was it?"

She worked for a casual tone. "Just a guy who's not my type. He asked me out before, and I thought he might again. I just wanted to let him down easy, letting him think I had a boyfriend."

He studied her, his eyes boring into hers. For a moment she worried he could see through the lie, but then he gave her an easy smile, his dimples popping up adorably in those rough stubbled cheeks. "I must be your type. That kiss—"

"Never happened."

He narrowed his eyes.

She glanced at the adjacent table, where several people were waiting to pay for their purchases with Cheryl. Apparently, the Missy and Ben make-out session had been quietly stepped around. She'd be more embarrassed except she'd do it again in a heartbeat. It had worked phenomenally well in getting Louis to back off. And, she could admit it, she'd enjoyed their kiss immensely, enough to be sorely tempted by Ben. She hadn't been with anyone since Matt, five months now, and the chemistry she had with Ben was unlike anything she'd ever felt before. And that was just from a kiss! Her stomach dipped imagining skin on skin, the hot rush of—

The problem with Ben, she reminded herself firmly, was they'd end up thrown together a lot with all their mutual friends. If they hooked up, they'd have to see each other afterwards. He'd probably be like, "hey, ex-lover, don't mind me flirting with this other woman." Who would no doubt be one of her friends. Nope.

"Let me take care of your purchase," she told him. "Then I need to help Cheryl."

He said something under his breath and then walked to the other side of the table.

She ignored his grumbling, neatly folding the dark gray sweater he preferred, and then wrapping it in tissue paper and tucking it into a white box. After she told him the price, she pointed out his next stop. "There's a gift-wrapping station over by the beach paintings if you want to take care of that too."

He pulled a wad of twenty-dollar bills from his wallet. "Here."

She counted them out, way too much. She tried to give some back, but he crossed his arms, tucking his hands away. "This is too much, nearly double."

"Keep it. A donation to the church."

Her throat constricted. He had no idea how much good this money would do this Christmas. "Ben…" She couldn't get the words past the lump in her throat.

"What?" His tone was brusque.

She swallowed hard. "Thank you. It'll be put to good use."

"Good." Another one-word terse reply.

"Are you mad I made you kiss me?"

His lips twitched. "I'm not mad."

"You seem…not happy?"

He leaned close to her ear, his words hot against her skin. "When a gorgeous sexy woman lays a kiss on you like that, twice, and then gives you the cold shoulder, you might be a little not happy too."

She warmed at the compliment. She'd never been called gorgeous before, and coming from his gorgeous self—wow. "I'm sorry. I didn't mean to give you the cold shoulder."

He straightened. "Okay. So now what?"

"I really do need to get back to work. I'm sure I'll run into you again. Fate, right?"

He leveled her with a look of pure aggravation. "Right." He snagged his sweater and stalked off.

"Wait!"

He stopped, slowly turned, and looked at her expectantly.

"You forgot your jam!" She held it out to him.

He marched back to her, irritation written all over his face. "Thank you," he bit out, taking the jam.

"Bye and thanks again."

He stalked off, jam in one hand, sweater box tucked under his arm. She let out a soft sigh, watching him go before remembering herself and jumping in to help.

By the time the craft bazaar ended at five o'clock, Missy was proud to say it had been a huge success. Her goal to raise two thousand dollars had been met and then some. Twenty-three hundred dollars, all of it going to the Harper family—Rena with her three kids, ages six, eight, and ten. She was one of the women Missy helped through the women's hotline. Rena was starting over in an apartment in Clover Park after escaping her abusive husband. The church community had come together to make sure the Harper family had furniture and the basics, but Missy wanted to do something more. She wanted the kids' first Christmas in their new hometown to be special. They'd each escaped with only one suitcase of personal belongings, not wanting to alert the abuser that they were leaving for good. The kids needed continuity—a tree with decorations, presents, a special Christmas dinner—to keep their childhood intact. They needed to know everything they loved about Christmas would still be there for them even if some things had changed. Missy knew from personal experience how important it was for a kid to have something they could depend on when their world turned upside down.

She tucked the money she'd collected from each vendor into the metal cash box, locked it, and stored it under the table. All the vendors were packing up, and she jumped in to help. There was still a pile of men's sweaters, probably their worst-selling item. She pulled a large plastic container from under the table and piled them in there. She found herself smiling, looking at the bluebird of happiness sweater. She briefly considered getting it for Ben as a joke gift, but then decided he might take it the wrong way. Like she wanted to continue with more flirty stuff, bantering back and forth… kissing. She flashed hot at the memory. *Onetime thing.* She tossed a few more sweaters on top, covering up the birdy goodness.

She finished packing the remaining knits and checked if

anyone else needed help, but half of the volunteers had already left, and the rest were fine on their own. She went upstairs to the storage closet, grabbed a broom and dustpan, headed back downstairs, and got to work. It was the Saturday before Thanksgiving, a date she'd planned purposely so she could hit all the Black Friday sales for the Harpers. She wanted those kids to wake to the excitement of a pile of presents on Christmas morning, to believe that Santa was there for them more than ever, to know they were good kids on the nice list no matter what their dad had done.

"Bye," Cheryl called, her hands full with a container of knits.

Missy set the broom against the wall. "You want help getting that to your car?" The woman maintained a teased blond hairstyle, but she had to be at least seventy.

"No, thanks, Harry's here. He'll be down in a minute to haul the rest."

"Okay, thanks so much for your help today."

"You're welcome. Your boyfriend was cute. Mr. Leather Jacket."

Missy fought back a blush, sure Cheryl had seen them making out. "Oh, ha-ha, he's not my boyfriend."

Cheryl raised her brows up past her fluffy bangs. "Whatever you call it these days."

Missy waved that away, grabbed the broom, and went back to sweeping. She couldn't dwell on Ben. She had bigger problems. Louis might show up at her apartment again, trying to get her alone. She'd better not hang onto the cash long. She'd deposit it as soon as the bank opened Monday morning. Then on Black Friday, she'd pay for everything with her debit card. She never carried debt on a credit card and kept a month's worth of rent saved at all times just in case. She'd hung onto that just-in-case money, her safety net, for years. Her former teen runaway self needed it to feel secure.

By the time she finished sweeping, everyone had cleared out. She stopped for a moment, sweating, and pulled her sweater away from her body, fanning it a bit. She was thirsty too, but she wanted to finish the job first. She bent to grab the dustpan when she heard a noise behind her. She whirled, her heart thundering.

Louis was standing by her table, cash box in hand.

"No!" she shouted, racing toward him.

He met her halfway, shoving her sideways, the metal cash box slamming into her shoulder. She hit the floor and he took off for the stairs. She scrambled to her feet, chasing him and hollering the whole time. "Stop him! Somebody stop him!"

He had a head start and was fast. She ran up the stairs, her eyes glued to that cash box.

Father Munson appeared in the entryway. "What's the problem?"

He was too old to chase Louis down. She kept running, shoving open the heavy front door Louis had just slammed back at her. By the time she got to the parking lot, he was driving away.

Bitter tears stung her eyes. He could not win. Those kids would not suffer because of him.

Father Munson appeared at her side. "What happened? Who was that man?"

She shook her head. "No one. Everything's okay."

"Sure?"

She pasted on a smile. "Yes. I thought he'd forgotten his gifts, but I was mistaken."

Father Munson patted her shoulder. "I left a man in the confessional. I'd better get back."

She nodded and headed for her car, shame bringing bile to her throat. She'd brought the devil to their door. She should've just written Louis a check and got rid of him. Instead she'd stubbornly clung to her emergency savings for fear of becoming homeless again, like when she was a teen runaway living on the streets. Fear had controlled her once more. Dammit.

She swallowed down the bile. Her savings wasn't enough to repay the money he'd just stolen.

Everyone had worked so hard to make this event a success. Most of them had donated their profits entirely to the cause Missy had championed. She had to find a way to repay that money in time for Christmas.

Her fault. Her problem. No one had to know she'd ever been involved with such an awful man. Her ex would remain her shameful secret.

3

Four days later, Missy was riding in a limo with her friends in a dreamy haze. If you had told her back when she was on the streets, hungry and clawing her way through just to survive, that one day she'd be attending movie star Claire Jordan's *Fierce Loving* wrap party at a palatial mansion in the Connecticut countryside, she wouldn't have believed it. Claire was a Happy Endings Book Club member and star of the Fierce trilogy movies based on books written by former book club member Julia Marino. Everything good in Missy's life could be traced back to her connection with the Happy Endings Book Club, a romance book club she never would've joined on her own. She didn't even believe in a romantic happy ending. And that connection was all due to her younger sister, Lily Marino.

Three years ago, out of the blue, Missy got a call from a woman claiming to be her sister—both of them put up for adoption as babies from the same mother to different families. Missy had agreed to meet her, figuring at least someone would understand how much their biological mother sucked. They'd connected immediately, but it was only for a week. Missy had been living in Seattle at the time and thought she'd never see Lily again. But Lily kept in touch and, when Lily got engaged two months later, she asked Missy to be maid of honor, a huge step for their tentative relationship. Their bond strengthened during Missy's visit for the wedding, resulting in Missy moving to Clover Park. Lily's family by marriage, the Marinos, had welcomed Missy, giving her a job and leading her to the Happy Endings Book Club. The debt she owed the Marinos was immense. They made Clover Park feel like home.

She focused on her friends all dressed up for the special occasion. Lexi and Hailey sat across from her, Sabrina by her side. The rest of their friends from the Happy Endings Book Club had skipped the limo in favor of driving with their fiancés or husbands. Guess the limo crowd were the last of the single women in their group. Fine by Missy. Sisters before misters, forever and ever, amen.

Lexi's shoulder-length dark brown hair was swept into a sophisticated twist, her makeup flawless, and she wore a scandalously slit red dress, exposed from ankle to waist. For sure she was commando under that thing. Lexi was a lot like Missy—no-nonsense and practical.

"Champagne?" Lexi asked, passing the bottle over to Missy. Claire kept the limo stocked for them.

Missy took a slug from the bottle, delicately wiping some from her chin. She smiled at Lexi. "Looks like your dress ripped."

Lexi swished the bottom of her dress from side to side. "Eat your heart out, Blake Grenier!" He was the drop-dead gorgeous co-star of the Fierce trilogy movies.

"Or you," Missy quipped.

Everyone laughed.

Missy passed the champagne bottle to Sabrina, who huffed. "Where are the glasses? I can't show up to an A-list party in one of Claire's designer dresses with champagne spilled all over my front." Her full-length lavender dress was exquisite—frothy and light with lace and sheer panels. Her long dirty blond hair was smooth and glossy, her brown eyes accented by smoky eyeliner, even her round apple cheeks had more definition with makeup. Quite a transformation from girl-next-door to glam. Of course, she was still sweet as ever.

Missy felt a little plain next to Sabrina, wearing her usual little black dress, her brown hair not at all glossy or styled, just straight down to her shoulders. At least her push-up bra made it look like she had cleavage.

"So don't spill," Missy told Sabrina.

"I got it," Hailey said, sliding open a storage cabinet and pulling out a stack of plastic cups. Hailey somehow moved with ease in a black strapless dress that fit her like a glove. Probably from all her years on the beauty pageant circuit. She was a former beauty queen with long strawberry blond hair, pale blue eyes, and a flawless complexion. Now she worked as a wedding planner and was the leader of the Happy Endings Book Club.

Sabrina leaned forward and took the offered cup. "Thanks, Hailey. I have to be so careful. I'm sure this dress cost a fortune."

Hailey nodded. "It's classier to drink from a cup." Hailey was *always* classy.

Lexi showed off an exposed leg and purposely slurred her words. "What're you saying, we're not classy?"

Missy made a show of adjusting her strapless bra. "Yeah, we're classy!"

"Classy with a K," Sabrina said, which made Hailey laugh.

Hailey took them all in with a bright smile that meant she was shifting to hyper planner mode, her speech rapid-fire. "Anyone have time this weekend to help me get ready for the holiday stroll and tree decorating? There's still a lot to be done decoration-wise, plus the favors I'm preparing for the kids, the raffle, the gift-wrapping for seniors—did I tell you about that event? I merged the gift-wrapping thing into the tree-decorating event. I'm also on the hunt for miniature stockings for—"

"Hold that thought," Missy said. She turned to Sabrina. "Pass her the champagne." Hailey had always been driven, but ever since she'd become single, ending a long-term friends-with-benefits situation, she'd catapulted past driven to hyper. The real issue, they all privately agreed, was Josh

Campbell. The pair, previously involved in an escalating frenemy one-upmanship fueled by a palpable sexual chemistry, abruptly stopped all sparring when Josh got a girlfriend. Kind of a shame for the rest of them too because watching Josh and Hailey at Garner's Sports Bar & Grill, where they all hung out, was an extremely entertaining and frequent event. Josh was manager and bartender there and took great pleasure in denying Hailey her favorite drink as retaliation for whatever devious thing she'd come up with. The rumor that Josh had a tiny banana was only one example of Hailey's brilliant moves. Josh's new girlfriend was the anti-Hailey—a laid-back, supersweet, bohemian yoga instructor.

Sabrina handed the bottle to Hailey. "Sweetie, promise me you'll take a breather after the holidays." Sabrina was a relationship counselor with a deeply compassionate nature.

Hailey poured herself a glass, her smile bright. "I'm fine. This is what I do." She set the champagne bottle back in the ice bucket and lifted her cup. "To planning fantastic events!"

Missy and Sabrina exchanged a concerned look.

"I'm fine!" Hailey chirped. "Seriously, I've never been happier!"

"We totally believe you!" Lexi chirped back in a dead-on Hailey impersonation.

Hailey's pale blue eyes narrowed. "You've been snippier lately. When was the last time you had a man in your life?"

"Don't go there," Lexi said with no real heat.

Hailey lifted one shoulder. "It's what I do. I'm a happy-ending facilitator."

"The Love Junkie," Sabrina added with a straight face. "It says so on her card."

Hailey smiled serenely, proud of her self-appointed title. "And, Sabrina, you're getting quite a rep as a relationship healer."

Sabrina blushed. "It's a self-fulfilling prophesy. Word spreads and then more people looking for healing come to me. They're ready and willing to do the work."

Hailey flicked her long strawberry blond hair over her

shoulder. "We should put our heads together for some more coupling."

Lexi snorted. "*Coupling*. That sounds dirty."

They cracked up.

"What about you, Sabrina?" Hailey asked. "You're an expert on relationships, does that mean you'd like one for yourself soon?"

Sabrina blushed, looking away. "Sometimes when you know as much as I do, it's almost a curse." She turned back to Hailey. "I can see warning signs of relationship incompatibility a mile away. It makes it hard to relax and just enjoy."

"I could help you get comfortable," Hailey said. "I've brought so many couples together already, and some of them were seriously gun-shy."

Missy stifled a laugh. Hailey took credit for a lot of couples that they all thought would've happened anyway.

Sabrina pointed at Missy, purposely shifting Hailey's focus.

Hailey cocked her head at Missy. "What's so funny?"

Missy forced a straight face. "Nothing."

Hailey crossed her legs and leveled an assessing look at Missy. "How long have we known each other now? Two years? And in that time I don't think you've ever mentioned a man in your life."

Missy leaned forward. "That's because there is no man in my life *by choice*. Casual hookups, yes. Relationships, no."

The women went quiet. It was the first time Hailey had pressed Missy on her relationship status. Lexi and Sabrina already knew she preferred casual hookups. Missy had never explained why, and her friends had never asked, probably sensing her defensiveness on the matter. The only people who knew about Missy's past were her therapist back in Seattle and her sister. She'd wanted to start over in Clover Park, where nobody would ever know she was once a victim. She wanted to be a new Missy, a stronger, smarter version of herself. Her recent fuckup with the married Matt was still too humiliatingly fresh. Missy had learned the key to surviving was to address only the immediate danger and leave the emotional aftermath for later when she was ready.

She wasn't ready. She'd known better, and it still burned that she'd been stupid enough to let Matt in close.

"Can I ask why?" Hailey asked gently.

"This is a circle of trust," Sabrina added in such a serious tone Missy nearly laughed.

Lexi nodded. "Doesn't leave this limo."

Missy sighed, knowing her friends meant well. "Let's just say I've had too many bad experiences to ever trust a man." She thought about her ex-husband and all the women she'd personally helped, victimized like her. "And I don't mean just a bad breakup. I mean traumatically bad." At their sympathetic looks, her throat tightened, and a telltale stinging in her eyes told her to shut up. "Let's talk about something else. I've really been looking forward to this party, and I don't want to get all worked up about my shitty past experiences."

"Absolutely," Sabrina said. "Another time. Just know my door's always open." Sabrina lived down the hall from Missy.

"Mine too," Lexi and Hailey chimed in at the same time.

Missy blinked rapidly, her lips pressed tightly together.

"More champagne?" Hailey asked, breaking the tension. They all offered their glasses, and the mood immediately became lighter.

By the time they arrived at the mansion, they were all tipsy, having finished off a second bottle of champagne, and were getting increasingly raunchy, laughing like loons. They settled down as the limo pulled around a circular driveway with a marble fountain in the center. This place looked like someone took a European palace complete with manicured grounds and plopped it down in the middle of Connecticut. No wonder they filmed the movies here.

The driver opened the door for them and then helped them out of the limo. Sometimes Missy had to pinch herself that this was all real.

A distinguished-looking older man in a black tuxedo answered the door (a butler?) and took their coats for them. Hailey, always the confident leader, strode through the crowd of mingling people in the two-story foyer, bypassing the adjacent crowded parlor and dining room, and went straight back to the conservatory. The large white-paneled room had only two sofas, a couple of high-backed chairs, and a grand piano—probably cleared out for maximum mingling at the party. A crowd gathered by the bar on the opposite side of the room.

They quickly found Claire surrounded by admirers. Hailey didn't hesitate to join the group, coming right up to Claire with a beaming smile and warm congratulations. Claire still looked the part of her character, Mia, with shoulder-length brown hair instead of her natural blond. Claire hugged Hailey, and the rest of them slid in close.

"I'm so happy you're here!" Claire exclaimed, hugging each of them before addressing her group of admirers, saying, "These are my sisters from another mister! Seriously, they have been my rock through all three movies."

The group welcomed them, and Claire introduced each of them—part of her regular crew working for her production company. Then Blake Grenier—A-list movie star, featured player in every woman's erotic Fierce trilogy fantasies, and *People*'s Sexiest Man Alive—joined them. He was breathtaking in real life. His eyes were impossibly blue, accented by his dark blue custom-tailored suit and jet-black hair. His features were masculine perfection, strong and sharp, his lips sensuous. She'd swoon if she were the type. He positively oozed sex.

The crew went quiet at Blake's arrival for some reason. Everyone stared at him, Missy included.

Blake turned to Hailey. "I remember you," he said in a deep charming voice. "You stole the corporate party scene. I was sure you'd acted before." Some of her friends had been extras in the first movie.

Hailey smoothed her hair. "I do have a lot of pageant experience."

Blake flashed a wolfish smile. "I'd love to hear about it."

Claire shot a warning look at Hailey that she blithely ignored.

"Can I get you a drink?" Blake asked, gesturing to the bar at the far side of the room.

"I'd love one!" Hailey left with him.

Claire frowned and Missy shifted next to her to ask in a quiet voice, "Is he bad news?"

Claire nodded and whispered back, "He's just looking for a quick lay."

Missy lifted a shoulder. "Maybe she wants that."

"No way!" Claire exclaimed. "Hailey? She's a romantic. Her entire wedding planning business is based on her passion for romance."

Missy inclined her head. "She's been out of sorts. Let her enjoy the attention. I'll check on her in a bit."

Claire blinked rapidly. "Thanks, Missy. I know I can be a bit of a mother hen, but you ladies…" Her voice choked.

"I know," Missy said, her own throat tightening from the emotion she heard in Claire. Their group was tight, and Missy knew Claire especially appreciated that closeness because she found it hard to make real friends as a celebrity. Most people wanted something from her.

"I love you guys," Claire said, wiping a tear from under her eye.

Missy squeezed her arm. "We love you too."

Sabrina smiled and nodded. Lexi raised a fist in solidarity.

Claire let out a small laugh. "Sorry. I get a little emotional after a movie wraps. And this was a huge one. Three years, three movies, same cast, most of the same crew. They become like family. It's always hard to say goodbye."

Sabrina leaned in. "You'll always have us."

Claire lost it, breaking down in tears. Sabrina swooped in, putting an arm around Claire and guiding her away, talking quietly the whole time. As soon as Claire left, the group of admirers moved on.

"You want a drink?" Missy asked Lexi.

"I should probably eat first," Lexi said. "Let's find one of those tuxedoed waiters."

They did a tour of the downstairs, sampling the gourmet appetizers offered by the waiters. The best was stuffed mushrooms with crab and lobster. Finally, they returned to the conservatory, where Hailey and Blake were flirting up a storm in a quiet corner of the room.

She and Lexi stopped at the bar before settling close enough to keep an eye on Hailey without being obvious.

Mad, the youngest and only girl in the Campbell family, joined them in her black pants suit. The woman never wore a dress. "What the hell is she doing?" She inclined her head in Hailey's direction, her dyed fire-engine red hair flopping into her face. She shoved her hair away. "She knows he's an asshole that uses women."

"Maybe she's lonely," Lexi said.

"Maybe she wants him," Missy said. Hell, any woman with a pulse would want him.

Mad looked around and then confided with a small smile, "Maybe she wants to make Josh jealous."

They followed her gaze across the room, where Josh stood in a white button-down shirt with dark gray dress pants, an unusually dressy look for him, with a clear view of Hailey. Josh was tall with an athletic build, like all of the Campbell men, his dark brown hair on the longish side, giving him a sexy rumpled look. His casual laid-back charm was coupled with an edge that Missy thought moved him up the scale from good looking to seriously hot. He was a trained warrior, a former paratrooper in the army who'd dropped from a plane into enemy territory, where he'd prevailed in hand-to-hand combat. Missy and her friends had never pursued him because they all thought he was meant for Hailey, whether the two of them liked it or not. For now, Josh was with the bohemian Clarissa, standing in front of him in a deep blue sheath dress with white embroidered flowers, her long thin brown braids loosely pinned into a bun, her light brown skin glowing with good health. Clarissa's back was to Hailey, but she had to notice Josh looking over her shoulder, his attention fixated on someone else. And every time Josh looked over at Hailey, Hailey flirted even more.

"It's working," Missy said.

"Yeah," Mad said with a grin. "I feel better now. I thought

she was actually fooled by Blake's movie-star shine for a minute there. Later, bitches. Claire says she has a pizza for me in the kitchen."

"Oh, no, thanks, we're stuffed," Lexi said.

"You can have some too," Mad said belatedly. "Sorry. She got it special for me since I don't like this fancy stuff, but I'll share."

"Go ahead and enjoy," Missy said. "We're fine."

Mad strode away, her fiancé fell into step with her, and they headed off for pizza.

A few minutes later, Hailey and Blake made their way out of the conservatory, heading who knew where. Missy and Lexi followed a discreet distance behind, through the maze of people, all the way to the two-story foyer, where only a few people lingered. Missy and Lexi exchanged a look of alarm. Hailey was either leaving with Blake or heading up the huge staircase. Either way, they wouldn't be able to keep an eye on her.

"Where are you two heading?" Missy called.

Hailey stopped and turned. "Blake's giving me a tour. They shot some of the scenes upstairs."

"We'll go too," Missy said.

"Yeah, we're big fans of the Fierce trilogy," Lexi said.

Blake whispered something to Hailey.

Hailey nodded. She crossed to Missy and Lexi and pulled them aside. "Ladies, I'm fine. Really. Thank you for your concern."

Lexi leaned in. "He's gonna be out the door before you can get your panties back on."

"Like I'm wearing panties," Hailey said with a cheeky grin.

Lexi grinned. "Hey, me too."

Hailey's eyes widened. "I was kidding! Geez, Lexi, at least wear a thong!"

"Seriously," Missy said in a low voice, "is this what you want?"

Hailey sighed. "You think I haven't dealt with men like

him before? And maybe I'm up for it. I could use a breather, like Sabrina said."

Missy shook her head. "I think Sabrina meant some quiet meditation time."

"Or counseling time," Lexi said.

Hailey tossed her hair over her shoulder. "I don't need therapy. I just need to let loose."

"We'll be waiting right here for you," Lexi said.

"I'm fine." Hailey pasted on a smile, probably because she was getting irritated. She gave both their arms a squeeze, turned and headed back to Blake, who didn't look happy to be kept waiting.

Blake put a hand low on Hailey's back, guiding her toward the stairs. They'd only taken one step when Josh appeared suddenly in the foyer, his expression fierce.

He spoke in a stern commanding voice. "Hailey, no."

Hailey whirled. "What?"

Josh was not playing around. "Not him. Literally any other guy at this party, but not him."

"What's your problem?" Blake snarled.

"You, asshole." Josh hitched a thumb. "Now move along."

"Josh!" Hailey exclaimed. "You have no right—"

"Hailey, go," Josh ordered. "Back to the party."

Hailey's jaw dropped.

Clarissa appeared in the foyer. "Josh, what's going on?"

Josh's attention was riveted on Hailey. "*Now.*"

Hailey lifted her chin. "I will not. I'm going on a tour with Blake."

Josh's voice dropped, low and menacing. "No, you're not."

"I'll take care of this," Blake said, heading straight for Josh.

Josh held his ground, feet shoulder width apart, body tense in clear battle mode. The two men were equally matched in size, but Josh was far more dangerous.

The few lingering people in the foyer cleared out fast, probably because the men were circling each other and they didn't want to get caught in the fray. Hailey remained on the stairs, her gaze locked on Josh. Clarissa watched Josh too, one hand over her mouth, most likely concerned about how much trouble Josh would get in for damaging Blake.

Blake shoved Josh. In a flash, Josh had him pinned flat on his back, his knee in Blake's chest.

Blake's face was a mottled red. "One swing and I will sue you for everything you're worth!"

Josh got off him and took a step back. "Wouldn't get much."

Blake scrambled to his feet, his lip curling. "What do you want with Hailey?" He gestured toward Clarissa. "You've already got a hot piece—"

Josh slammed him against the wall. Blake struggled like mad to get free.

"Josh!" Clarissa and Hailey exclaimed in near unison.

Josh threw Blake to the side. "Stay away from her."

Blake stumbled and straightened. "Which her? Can't decide? Let me make it easy." He came back at Josh, swinging. Josh didn't try to duck or block the punch; instead he rammed into Blake, taking him to the ground. Fists flew—the men a blur of motion.

Lexi muttered, "I'll get Jake," and ran off to find Josh's identical twin. Smart. Jake could get through to him.

Missy bit her lip. They needed a couple of strong guys to pull these two apart. She glanced around, and the front door opened. Ben and Logan, Josh's youngest brother, stepped inside.

"Guys!" she called urgently. "Break them up before someone gets hurt."

"Shit," Logan said. "Is that Josh?"

"Yes!" Missy exclaimed. "And Blake Grenier!"

He and Ben rushed forward to break them up. Ben headed for Josh, and just before he could grab him, Logan hollered, "Not from behind!"

Too late. Ben put a hand on Josh's shoulder from behind, Josh grabbed Ben's hand, twisted, and then Ben was flat on his ass. "It's me!" Ben shouted as Josh loomed over him. "Ben!"

Josh quickly backed off, low and scanning the room for more threats, a warrior in battle, his eyes deadly calm. Blake was on the floor at Logan's feet. Threat neutralized.

Logan looked down at Blake. "You're lucky he wasn't serious about kicking your ass."

Blake flushed bright red and stood, knocking Logan's shoulder before leaving, slamming the front door behind him.

Lexi rushed in with Jake, who approached Josh, speaking quietly to him. Their heads together, the twins were nearly indistinguishable. Josh shook his head. Jake kept talking until Josh shrugged him off and pulled away.

Clarissa crossed her arms and announced, "I want to go home."

Josh went over to her. "I'm fine. I'm calming down."

Clarissa frowned. "I'm not. Take me home."

"Okay, I'll take you home." Josh lifted a hand in a small goodbye, his expression hard. They left.

The front door closed behind them, and Hailey stared at it for a moment, her lips pressed tightly together, before rushing from the room.

Missy and Lexi exchanged an incredulous look. Neither of them had ever seen Josh truly mad and never to the point of a physical confrontation.

"Holy shit," Lexi said.

"Men," Missy said.

Lexi looked over Missy's shoulder. "I'm going to check on Hailey."

"I'll catch up with you." She turned toward Ben, who was standing now and taking off his black leather jacket, looking all sexy and pissed off.

She couldn't resist.

4

"Ben Wright, this must be fate!" the woman who haunted his erotic dreams declared. "You flat on your ass in the very same foyer of a party I'm attending."

"You again," Ben grumbled. "That's what I get for trying to help. Knocked on my ass and mocked by a pseudo-brunette."

Missy pursed her luscious lips. "It's not polite to mention a woman's dye job."

He shrugged. "It's not polite to mention a man's flat on his ass."

She bit back a smile, clearly enjoying his unheroic fall.

Logan stopped by his side. They were as close as brothers, having grown up together, and were now business partners at Checkin, an online service that did background checks on personal caregivers and short-term contractors. Logan looked like a younger, wiry version of Josh, if Josh had light brown hair and a beard. His eyes held a hint of amusement. "I told ya not to approach him from behind. You know he's got hair-trigger reflexes, wired for battle."

Ben blew out a breath. "I know. I wasn't thinking. I pulled back at the last minute and just put my hand on his shoulder instead of grabbing him and hauling him off."

"You would've been hurting if you'd grabbed him."

Logan turned to Missy. "You see the whole thing? What the hell set him off?"

Missy grimaced. "Hailey was about to go upstairs with Blake Grenier."

Logan shook his head. "Josh has a great girlfriend. So what if Hailey's with Blake?"

"Grass is always greener," Ben put in.

"Or maybe he has unresolved feelings for Hailey," Missy said in a patient tone. Like she had to explain the intricacies of male-female relationships to the men. Raised by a single mom and then his grandmother, Ben was clued in to the subtle undercurrents women put out.

Logan threw his hands up. "You can't talk to him about it. I've tried. He doesn't want to want Hailey, and he'll take your head off for even mentioning he should just get her out of his system."

"Why doesn't he want to want her?" Missy asked.

Logan got quiet before saying, "You should ask him about it." Logan took the two of them in. "It's kinda sad, isn't it?"

"Bah." Ben socked Logan's arm in a reassuring gesture. "He'll be fine."

"I'm going in," Logan said, inclining his head toward the party noise.

"I'll catch up," Ben said.

Logan lifted a brow, a smile playing over his lips. "Is that so?"

"Get out of here." Ben shoved his shoulder, and Logan walked off with a laugh. Ben turned to Missy, taking in her tight black dress with cleavage on full display. His mouth went dry. Her waist was small, her hips curvy, toned legs, and black high heels. He forced his gaze back to her beautiful face, his voice rough. "So here we are again."

"I told you we'd keep running into each other. The web is too thick to escape."

He blinked. "The web?"

She waved airily. "Your friends, my friends, all the vows of forever."

He rolled on the balls of his feet. "Yeah, that seems to be going around."

A butler guy appeared out of nowhere. "May I take your coat, sir?"

"Sure." He handed it over, and the guy disappeared to wherever he came from. There were probably secret tunnels in an old palace like this.

Missy cocked her head. "You don't buy into it?"

He did a quick rewind. Oh, yeah. The guys getting shackled. "Do you?"

"No."

He relaxed. Now this was someone he could have some fun with. No worries about future demands of commitment. "I don't believe in marriage."

"The institution? Interesting. Why not?"

"I've never seen a good one. Have you?"

"My sister."

"I guess there are exceptions," he allowed.

"What about your friends?"

"Remains to be seen. Early days yet."

Her brown eyes lit with amusement. "You're a true pessimist, aren't you?"

He gave her his dimpled smile, pouring on the charm. "Not at all. I just need to see it to believe it."

"Darn. I'm a glass half empty kind of person."

"My condolences."

She laughed.

He leaned close, breathing in her floral scent. He loved that she smelled so girly when she talked so tough. "If fate keeps bringing us together, maybe we should stop resisting."

She rolled her eyes. "Come on, let's get back to the party."

"Not so fast. Don't even try to tell me you didn't feel something during our incredibly hot make-out session."

She looked up at him, completely unfazed. "You looking to get laid?"

Yes. "Missy, I'm offended."

She shrugged one shoulder. "No big deal. An itch you need to scratch once in a while, right?"

He was speechless. Had he really just met the perfect woman? Casual sex, fun and flirty banter, no commitment. She was ringing every bell. *Ding! Ding! Ding!*

She continued in her practical wonderful way. "I normally would say bring it on, but we know too many of the same people. It would be so awkward to keep running into each other."

Damn. It was all sounding so good until the "but."

"Awkward," he echoed.

"Yeah."

He took her hand. "What if it wasn't awkward?" He could be very smooth and, if she would just keep on being practical, they could have a lot of fun.

She pulled her hand from his. "You seem harmless, but…"

I'll see your but and raise my but! "Well, I am harmless, but I feel a little dirty now."

"I didn't realize you were so delicate. Forget I said anything."

"I can't forget it."

"Whatever."

He wanted her bad. No way around it. "How about…" He trailed off as her phone rang and she pulled it from her tiny purse.

He waited while she spoke in a smooth professional tone, then hung up, and smiled. "Work stuff?" he asked.

"Yeah. I'm only working mornings at my regular job. I'm an admin at a construction company, and this is their slow season. Anyway, I just wanted to pick up some extra cash for the holidays. Now I can. I start the day after Thanksgiving."

He read between the lines. "Things are tight? How much do you need?" Checkin was doing so well they were looking for investors to take it to the next level. He could easily help her out.

"I'm fine," she said firmly, her expression tight. "Just for a little gift spending."

In that instant he knew everything was not "fine." His natural impulse to help a woman in need made him consider offering her a job instead of a handout. He sensed she'd respond better to that, and they could use an admin at Checkin. Theirs would be out until after the New Year. Patty's daughter just had her first baby and she'd gone up to Vermont to be with her. The filing had been piling up, and he and Logan hadn't done any of the data entry for weeks now.

He clamped his mouth shut. If Missy worked for him, with this intense attraction, it would be like shooting himself in the foot. Why put temptation in front of him every day for weeks that he *absolutely* could not act on? It would hurt Checkin's chances with investors if it looked like he had a pattern of acting inappropriately with women he employed. Not that he ever had, but his reputation already had a blemish on it through no fault of his own.

Six months ago, Ben had helped out a college friend by hiring his cousin Ashley to work sales and marketing for Checkin. It didn't work out. After three months with zero results, Ben let her go. Then she accused him of sexual harassment. He'd been sick over it. That was not him, and if his mother had been alive to hear about it, he would've died of shame. He'd been raised to treat women with respect and he did. He was a total professional. He'd never even been alone with her. Half the time she worked from home and probably hadn't even been working. Logan had loyally stood by him. Eventually, Ben was cleared of all charges, but the damage was done. His reputation was sullied even to have been accused and, if he was really honest, it changed him too. He was a lot more mistrustful of women in general.

The harassment charge was his dark secret, though word had leaked out through some business channels, which was the whole reason Logan was taking the lead for the investor meetings in January.

He gave Missy a small smile. "Good luck with your new job. What'll you be doing?"

Missy's cheeks flushed pink. "Uh, just a temp job."

"What kind of temp job?" he asked, curious why she was blushing.

She cleared her throat before mumbling, "Customer service."

"Get in here!" Claire exclaimed, appearing in the foyer. "Jake and I have a big announcement."

"Coming!" Missy called, sounding immensely relieved. Odd.

He followed her through the house toward the sound of a crowd. "Think she's pregnant?" he asked Missy under his breath.

"Wouldn't be surprised," Missy said.

They reached the back of the house, where a large conservatory was filled with people. Claire stood on a chair, and Jake whistled loudly, bringing a hush to the room. Claire looked down at him. "Thanks, honey." She stretched her arms wide and beamed. "Jake and I bought a house in Connecticut with land for horses—"

"And dogs!" Jake put in.

"Yes!" Claire said on a laugh. "And dogs. And hopefully kids soon, though I'm not pregnant—"

"Yet!" Jake held up a finger. "Though we're practicing every chance we get."

"Jake!"

He grinned, looking up at her adoringly. "What?"

Claire shook her head at him, smiling. "It's only a half hour away from Clover Park, and I cannot wait to have everyone over. We move in January."

Missy and her friends cheered the loudest.

"Oh, that's so nice," Missy said in a breathy choked voice. "A family and home." She rushed forward, where her friends had gathered around Claire, the women exclaiming excitedly to finally have Claire living nearby. She normally travelled all over the world to her movie locations. Sounded like she and Jake were putting down roots, settling down.

Ben couldn't imagine that life for himself. He knew all too well the pain of losing someone close, with his mom's long battle with cancer, and never wanted to feel that kind of pain again. Missy seemed really choked up about the family and home thing. She'd said she didn't believe in long-term. Now he wasn't so sure if he believed her.

~

The homeless shelter in South Norfolk, a forty-minute drive from Clover Park, was new for Missy yet familiar at the same time. Cinder-block walls, cheap vinyl flooring, the long communal tables in the dining room, the smell of disinfectant in the air. None of it said "home" to her, but it had been her salvation as a teen living on the streets, running low on cash and food.

She'd met other teen girls who'd turned to prostitution to survive, but she couldn't stomach the idea. She'd run away at fifteen to escape her new "uncle," a man who believed living in the same house made her fair game. Her aunt hadn't protected her, probably because she resented being her guardian after Missy's parents died. Missy had made her peace with it. Her early life—orphaned at ten, running away at fifteen, bouncing through shelters and then foster homes, married young to an abusive husband, all of that hell—had only made her stronger. She knew beyond a doubt she could take care of herself, knew she was a survivor. And she gave back so other people in similar difficult circumstances would know they could survive too.

Normally she volunteered at church on Thanksgiving for the handful of people who showed up there for a hot meal, but this year the church had decided to bring the hot meals to the few people who needed them. She went straight to the kitchen for her three to seven p.m. shift. The place was already abuzz with activity. She quickly located the sign-in and was greeted warmly by a woman in her fifties wearing a canary yellow track suit, her dark hair neatly tucked into a hairnet.

"Hi, I'm Missy Higgins, reporting for the three to seven shift."

"Nice to meet you, Missy. I'm Leah. Did you book your volunteer appointment ahead of time? We're all booked up for the day."

"Yes."

"Excellent." She picked up a clipboard with the sign-in

sheet and located Missy's name, checking it off. "You can tuck your things in the closet." She gestured toward the back of the kitchen. "Grab an apron and hairnet. We start serving at five." Leah looked around the busy space. "We'll put you on potato duty."

"You got it."

Missy quickly stored her coat. She'd skipped the purse, preferring only the basics in her back jeans pocket. Not that everyone at the shelter was a thief, but desperate people sometimes did desperate things. She didn't judge anyone for where they were at. Survival was an instinct and one she'd felt on a primal level as a teen.

She reported for potato duty a few minutes later, apron and hairnet in place. A young couple were already at work peeling the potatoes and setting them in large metal bowls. "Hi, I'm Missy, your potato-duty helper."

"I'm Hannah," the woman with purple hair in two low pigtails said. "This is Jackson. Could you wash and dry some more potatoes for us? We're on a roll here with the peeling. Sacks of potatoes are along the far wall."

"Yup." She hauled a large sack of potatoes to the prep sink, set down some paper towels, and grabbed a scrub brush. Soon she got into a rhythm, the sound of the running water and the repetition of scrub and rinse putting her into a nearly Zen state. So when a masculine voice said, "I'll dry," she nearly jumped out of her skin.

He laughed. "Sleeping on your feet?"

Her heart still pounding, she turned and met Ben's mischievous blue eyes. Maybe fate really was putting him in her path. He was here of all places, smelling like fresh soap and warm spice, looking more gorgeous in a hairnet than any man had a right to. His lips curved into a dimpled smile that made her knees weak.

"You do remember me, don't you?" Ben asked in a teasing voice. "I didn't dye my hair like some people."

"What're you doing here?" she asked softly.

"I always come here on Thanksgiving." He grabbed some paper towels and began efficiently drying potatoes and putting them in a large plastic bowl. "It was a tradition with my mom."

She bobbed her head and went back to work, having a weird out-of-body experience, staring down at herself and Ben volunteering together on Thanksgiving Day. He had depth, love for his family, caring for others less fortunate. He wasn't just a gorgeous flirt. He was the total package. All of these thoughts floated through her mind before she returned to reality, suddenly hyperaware of him. His tall, muscular build made her feel safe not wary like she sometimes was with men. His gray Henley with the sleeves pushed up, jeans that molded to his frame, the way he moved—all of it said he was comfortable in his own skin. He seemed tough enough to handle her, not needing the sweetness and light men seemed to prefer in a woman. And he was so, so sexy. She rapidly dismissed every reason why she couldn't have him and then just as quickly reversed it. He was making her nuts.

"No joke about this fate business?" he asked.

She forced a laugh even as the hair on the back of her neck stood at attention. It *did* feel like fate, and she didn't even believe in fate. She secretly laughed at people who believed in such a ridiculous thing. A magical force bringing people together? Ha! Yet it felt right. Every instinct in her body pointed toward him.

"You okay?" he asked.

Her natural defensiveness melted at the real concern in his voice. "I'm good, thanks. Is your mom here too?"

He stared at the potatoes. "No. She, uh, passed."

"Oh, I'm so sorry. I didn't mean to bring up a painful reminder."

He met her eyes, his voice gruff with emotion. "It's okay. It was a while ago. She died of brain cancer after a ten-year battle." He cleared his throat. "I was fifteen."

A jolt went through her. She'd been fifteen when her life took a turn for the worse too, running away from home. "I'm sorry. That must've been hard."

He nodded. "She was a social worker, true heart of gold.

Anyway, she always volunteered here, so I do too. In a way, it's like she's here with me."

Her eyes got hot. She was not a crier, but he'd shared from the heart, and that touched her deeply. Throat tight, she turned off the water, facing him while she reached deep down for a rare sharing of confidences. "I get that. I go to church because it reminds me of my parents. They died when I was ten in a car accident. I was at a friend's house."

His expression softened, his voice sympathetic. "Sorry to hear it." He paused before saying quietly, "I know that pain never really goes away. You just learn to live with it."

Her chest ached in this rare moment of connection with someone who really understood the deep pain of loss. She had the strangest impulse to hug him, lifting her hands as she leaned a little closer and then pulling back, dropping her hands.

He squinted at her. "Were you about to hug me?"

Her cheeks burned furiously, mortified to be caught in an awkward hug impulse. "No."

"I don't mind. Here, I'll start." He opened his arms to her.

She hesitated only a moment before wrapping her arms around his waist, giving him a small squeeze. His arms wrapped around her back in a warm hug that made her feel surrounded by pure radiant love. She didn't question it, only soaked it in.

"We could use some more potatoes down here!" Jackson called.

Missy jerked away from Ben.

"Shut up, Jackson," Hannah said. "They were having a moment."

"Sorry to hold up the line," Ben called, passing a couple of bowls of potatoes down to them.

Missy stood there, frozen. She'd shared too much, exposed herself.

Ben waved a hand in front of her face. "Stop your daydreaming and get back to work, Missy." He grinned. "It sounds like I'm calling you lowercase missy, but you are Missy. Melissa, right?"

She gave herself a mental shake. "Yes, Benjamin."

"It's Benward."

She stared at him.

He grinned. "Kidding. It's Benjamin."

She turned the water back on and scrubbed and scrubbed and scrubbed. If she kept talking, she feared she'd blurt her entire life story right here in the middle of a busy kitchen full of strangers. He'd shared, so she shared. No more. She didn't want to dwell on the past. She only ever shared like that with her sister, the most nonjudgmental loving person Missy had ever met.

"Wanna switch?" Ben asked. "I wash, you dry."

"No, I'm good."

"There's ten more sacks of potatoes plus more in the back."

"Check in with me in an hour."

A few minutes passed in silence before Ben said, "Cranberry-sauce duty is a lot more fun. Just some stirring and it smells so good."

She kept scrubbing potatoes and passing them over. "Then what're you doing over here on potato duty?"

"Why do you think I'm over here on potato duty?"

A shiver went down her spine. Her? He'd chosen the worst chore in the place because of her?

"I don't know," she finally said.

"You're dense."

She glared at him. "I am not."

"Duh."

"Oh, that's real mature." She went back to scrubbing.

"Missy Higgins," he said in a mock offended voice, "I am not leaving here today until you admit it's fate that brought us together. It's happened too much to be coincidental." His voice took on a deep robotic tone. "Resistance is futile."

She shook her head, focused on her chore. "You seriously believe in fate?"

"Not until you."

Shiver upon shiver, goose bumps on top of goose bumps. She risked a look at him, and he gazed back steadily with no hint of dimpled amusement. Her breath caught. She swore and went back to work. He chuckled in a deep rumble by her side.

Harmless flirt, harmless flirt, she repeated to herself in a mantra, though she was beginning to believe Ben was much more dangerous to her carefully structured safe life than that.

They fell into an easy rhythm, working another hour on potatoes before switching over to assembling stuffing ingredients in large pans. Ben kept up the conversation, asking about her job and telling her about his and Logan's company Checkin, a background-check service for employers. How she wished her current employer had used their service before hiring Matt last spring; then Missy would've known he was married. For sure she'd suggest they use it going forward. They often had to add a crew of short-term contractors for big jobs.

The dinner hour arrived, and she and Ben worked side by side at the hot-food station, serving up food to the long line of people. They talked little, but she was tuned in to him. He made eye contact with every single person he served, speaking in a warm friendly voice, even to some of the surly old men, and he joked around with the kids. Her heart just about burst. His mom must've set a tremendous example for him. Or maybe he inherited her compassionate nature. Either way, she knew how rare that was in people, and it made her admire him even more.

Dinner finished serving at seven, which was also when her shift ended.

"You up for cleanup?" Ben asked, heading back to the kitchen with her. "I'll wash this time. You dry."

"Sure," she said, even though she was tired from being on her feet. If Ben had more to give, then she could too.

She joined him at a sink full of soaking pots and large pans. "Wow, that's a lot of scrubbing."

"I've got the muscle power." He grabbed a scrub pad and got to work. "Many hands make light work," he said with a wink. "My mom used to say that."

Missy grabbed a dish towel. "You must've inherited her heart-of-gold gene, with all your selfless volunteering."

"Actually, I'm adopted, but thanks."

She couldn't breathe for a moment. The similarities in their paths were too glaring to ignore.

"You're volunteering too," he said. "Don't sell yourself short." He handed her a pot.

She took it and somehow fumbled it, the pot hitting the floor with a clatter. They both went to pick it up at the same time. Down on one knee, mirror images of each other, their gazes locked.

Ben handed the pot to her. "You must be getting tired," he said gently.

"I was adopted too," she whispered. "As a baby. It was my adoptive parents who died."

His eyes widened. "Me too, all of it." He rubbed his exposed forearm covered in goose bumps.

She bit her lip.

He reached for her elbow and guided her up with him. "What're the odds?" he asked, shaking his head.

"I know," she managed, a slight tremor in her voice. It was both freaky and comforting at the same time. He knew what it was like to live with the knowledge your mother gave you up. He knew what it meant to have a good adoptive family and then lose them. Their similar histories seriously made her believe in the mystical, a force greater than herself at play here. He just *might* be the only person on the planet who really got her.

Several minutes passed in silence while they worked, except for the din of other volunteers' conversations as dishes were scraped and piled into dishwashers or set in sinks to soak.

She studied his profile, his short light brown hair emphasizing his masculine features, sharp cheekbones, straight nose, lightly stubbled jaw. He turned, giving her a warm look that said *fate*. She heard it just like he'd said it out loud, and it was really starting to freak her out.

Maybe they weren't all that similar. Maybe his dad was

there for him the whole time and he hadn't felt alone like she had as a kid.

"Is your dad still around?" she asked.

He handed her a pot. "He split when I was two, so it was just me and Mom for a real long time. But Joe Campbell was an honorary dad. Mom set me up with the Police Athletic League on his baseball team. She knew Joe was a good man with a lot of sons. She wanted me to have that male influence."

She swallowed hard. They were spookily similar. She kept asking questions, needing to know if they'd actually lived parallel lives. "Then, later, your grandmother took you in?" She figured it must've went down that way because he was close with her. Missy had made the mistake of immediately sending a letter to her biological mom, asking her to take her in after her adoptive parents died. She had her mom's address from the birthday cards she'd sent. Missy never heard back. Her parents hadn't made a will, so the court appointed her adoptive mom's sister to take her in, who made it clear she was doing Missy a big favor, all while bitterly lamenting how little money social services provided for her care. The small proceeds from her parents' estate were squandered by her aunt before Missy ever saw a cent. She pushed that dark memory away, realizing Ben was talking.

"I'm sorry," she said. "I missed that last part. Did you say your grandmother moved into your place, or did you have to move to hers?"

"The first. But my family always felt bigger than that with the Campbells and all the other strays like me that hung around their house. I was one of the younger boys—Ty, Alex, me, and Logan. Parker was our age too, but he came along later."

"So you were happy?" she asked.

He lifted one corner of his mouth. "I take happiness where I can find it."

"That's smart."

"What about you?"

She shrugged, not willing to share any more of her tumultuous early life. "Like you, I take happiness where I can find it."

He went back to scrubbing a pot. She went back to drying.

A few minutes later, he handed her the next pot to dry. "What're you doing after this?"

"Why?"

He leaned close, giving her a sexy smile. "Because I'd like to do whatever you're doing."

Heat surged through her, her pulse skyrocketing. "I was planning on a hot bath with a glass of wine."

He winked. "It's smart to conserve water." He went back to work, whistling to himself.

She didn't know what to say. She wanted him, no question, but something held her back. She felt like she was on a high wire with no idea how she got there, unsure if it made more sense to retreat or rush forward and risk the fall. But then he made it easy for her.

"I've got an idea," he said. That mischievous look was back in his eyes, dimpled smile on full display. "How about tomorrow we jet off to Vegas for a long weekend. What happens in Vegas—"

She cooled. "I hate Vegas."

"How can you hate a playground?"

"Because it's my biological mother's playground. She's a dancer, and I use the term loosely."

He glanced at her, a light of surprise in his eyes, but no judgment. "Okay, so no Vegas." He washed a tray, rinsed, and handed it to her.

"Anyway, I don't have money for frivolous trips."

"I would've covered you."

She clenched her jaw. "I pay my own way." Paying her own way meant she was in charge of her life, taking care of herself. No man would ever hold the purse strings again no matter how enticing the offer.

He blew out a breath, but refrained from commenting. Smart man. She supposed, being raised by his mom and grandmother, he knew how to avoid land mines of conversation. She liked that. She didn't have the patience to bring a guy up to speed on woman speak.

They resumed working in silence. The tension was thick in the air—do-or-die moment fast approaching. If she turned him down now, after all they'd shared, he wasn't ever coming back. On the other hand, if they went somewhere together, well, what was the worst that could happen? Something heavy, deep, a relationship. But he'd said he didn't believe in long-term commitment. In fact, hadn't he said he didn't believe in the institution of marriage? In which case, he would expect something casual and light. That might work.

But then what about after the casual and light with all their mutual friends?

She watched him. His big, bulky-with-muscle, masculine self competently tackling a domestic chore. He was exceptional.

Maybe just for tonight. One night.

When they finished all the dishes, Ben dried his hands and turned to her, plucking his hairnet off and then hers. "This hair," he said, staring at her hair, "such a shame. All that gorgeous red. You hardly ever see a natural redhead."

She rolled her eyes, took off her apron, and made her way over to the laundry basket near the back door, tossing it in.

Ben followed her, wadding up his apron and throwing it in like a basketball. "Will you ever go back to red?"

She sighed. "I look like my biological mother with red hair. That's why I hate it. Every once in a while, I let it go natural, but then I can't stand it. I also got her big lips, but I'm stuck with those."

Ben stared at her mouth. "Missy, that mouth. Swear to God it's the sexiest thing I've ever seen."

She put her fingers to her lips. "But—"

"Trust me." He leaned down to her ear to whisper, "That mouth has starred in some very erotic dreams of mine."

She scowled, not at all appeased. "See? I have porn-star lips."

He traced the dip in her upper lip with his index finger

before pressing on her plump lower lip. "You have luscious sweet lips I want to feast on."

Her lips parted on a soft exhale. He smiled but made no move to kiss her. Instead, he dropped his hand, his gaze moving from her lips to her hair. "Do you still see your Vegas mom?" he asked.

"No."

"Then why does she get to decide how you wear your hair?"

"Why do you get to decide?" she returned.

His eyes danced with amusement. "You're a prickly one." He went to the closet and pulled out his black leather jacket, pulling it on. "I'll call you cactus from here on out."

She found her black wool coat and shoved her hands in the sleeves, irritated by the nickname, probably because it hit a little close to home. Her defenses sprang right up when someone pushed her. "Let me guess, you normally call your women sweetie or honey bunny."

He laughed out loud. "Honey bunny, that's a good one. No, I call them by their name. Maybe throw in a—" he dropped his voice, low and husky "—sexy thing if it's warranted."

Her cheeks heated, her neck too, and so many more southerly parts. "We should say goodbye to Leah."

"Sure, she's an honorary aunt. She was close with my mom."

She swallowed hard, his openness about his loss bringing a visceral deep empathy. She bumped his shoulder in a small gesture of affection, drawing a smile from him that reached his eyes, warm and tender. She wobbled for a moment, not used to warm and tender, before she walked over to where Leah was busy wiping down the counter. Ben followed close behind.

"We're heading out," Missy said. "Have a happy Thanksgiving."

Leah put the sponge down and gave Missy a warm smile. "You too, sweetheart. Thanks so much for your help." She turned to Ben. "There's my Super Ben. Your mom was looking down on you from heaven today."

"Super Ben to the rescue," he murmured. "I felt her."

Leah nodded, her eyes shiny, before giving him a hug. She pulled away and said to Missy, "This guy is a keeper. Good people."

"Aww, thanks," Ben said. "High praise from my aunt always gives me a boost with the ladies."

"Oh, you!" Leah said, cackling and shaking her head.

"Bye," Ben said, kissing Leah on the cheek. He took Missy's hand, surprising her, his larger hand enveloping hers in a firm clasp as he guided her through the kitchen and out to the dining room. She wasn't much of a hand holder, wasn't used to affectionate gestures at all, really. A hug here and there. Sex, yes. Hand holding, no. Before she could decide how she felt about it, they were on the front sidewalk and he let go.

"Welp..." She rocked back and forth on the balls of her feet, not sure how to finish that sentence. Goodbye? Come over? It's been real?

Ben closed the distance between them, instantly spiking her temperature despite the chilly November night. He pushed her hair back over her ear before gazing directly into her eyes, his voice gentle. "Tell me what you want."

"Nothing," she whispered. She never dared want anything. She got what she needed and that was enough.

His big hand cradled her jaw, tipping her face up to his. "What can I offer you is a better question."

That was a better question. Something she could handle. She licked her lips and he watched the movement. "If you're offering what I think you're offering..."

His thumb stroked her cheek. "I am."

She swallowed, her stomach fluttering, on that high wire again, terrified of falling. "One night."

"One night," he agreed. "And no spending the night."

It was everything she'd hoped for—clear-cut boundaries, passion with no hard feelings after. A little voice in her head warned it couldn't possibly be that easy, but she was done denying herself. "Deal."

He dipped his head, brushing his lips against hers. "How about we start tonight?" He kissed her for real then, his mouth hungry and hot, his arms wrapping around her, pulling her against his hard body and intoxicating heat. She wrapped her arms around his neck and kissed him back, pressing closer, needing more of him, not caring about anything but the raw animal instinct that drove her. Sex, that was all it was. Yes, yes, yes.

He pulled away so suddenly she lost her balance. He steadied her, then took her hand in his, this time entwining his fingers with hers as they walked to the parking lot. She decided she liked holding hands with Ben. She liked it a lot.

She couldn't wait to find out what else she liked with him.

5

———

Forty-five minutes later, she pulled her car into the driveway of Ben's house in Fieldridge, a town not far from Clover Park and dotted with horse farms and small clusters of homes, ranging from older ranch homes to elegant mansions perched high on the hill. Ben had a newer home, near the bottom of the hill, in a development full of cul-de-sacs, the kind of neighborhood with families, where kids could play in the streets and bike safely. She'd suspected he was well off, but the house confirmed it. His business must be doing fantastic because she knew he came from modest beginnings. A single mom on a social worker's salary couldn't afford a lot of luxury. Her respect and admiration for him went up several more notches. Her heart kicked up speed, a warning not to get too close.

Nope, not gonna happen. This was sex, nothing more. One night.

She calmed, following him inside through a spotless laundry room to a large gourmet kitchen with gleaming stainless steel appliances, white marble counters, and sleek white cabinets. He took off his jacket and hung it on a peg in the short hallway between the kitchen and laundry room. Then he helped her off with her coat and hung hers next to his.

"You want a drink?" he asked, heading toward the cabinets.

She stood next to the marble island, waiting for what they were both here for. "No, thanks."

He helped himself to a glass of water and took a long drink, watching her over the rim. "You want to watch a movie?"

"Not really."

"Hungry? I've got some leftovers from my early Thanksgiving with my grandmother. She eats at noon, naps by three."

She was hungry, but that could wait. "Maybe later."

He set his glass on the counter. "Give me a clue here. I'm good, but I'm not that good." He closed the short distance between them and tapped her head. "Can't read minds."

She looked up at him. "Maybe we could eat after sex."

He stared at her mouth, his voice rough. "So you're just here for sex."

"Aren't you?"

"Well, yeah, but—"

"I don't need all the niceties." She wrapped her arms around his neck. "Just fuck me."

His arm banded around her waist, pulling her tight against him, heat in his eyes. "Now you're speaking my language."

"It's all men's language."

His brows creased for a moment, staring at her like he was trying to read her soul. Fuck that. She kissed him roughly.

He growled deep in his throat and lifted her, setting her on the island, his mouth sealed over hers. His tongue invaded, his large hand cupping the back of her head, the other hand sliding down her back to cup her ass. He ground himself against her, all of him hard and hot, hitting just the right spot, pleasure spiraling out from her core. Something in her snapped, wild for him like she'd never been for any man. She bit his bottom lip, then sucked it, her nails digging into his shoulders, her hips rising to meet him in open invitation.

He pressed on her chin, easing her mouth open, pulling

back to stare at her for a moment before he closed the distance, his tongue tracing her lips. Then he surprised her, biting her lower lip hard enough to sting, jolting her. He sucked gently, soothing the sting, then grazed his lips over hers, bringing hot tingles over her sensitized lips.

She yanked his shirt over his head, sliding her hands over the hard planes of his body, reveling in the lines of his muscular shoulders to his warm chest to flat stomach. He tossed his shirt behind him and then ripped her shirt off. She grabbed his head and kissed him, rough and hungry, her body humming in anticipation, and he met her there, the intensity skyrocketing. His hands were on her bra, working to get it off, while she rapidly undid the button and zipper on his jeans. And then she had him in hand, thick and hard, stroking him.

He swore, finally got the bra free, tossed it and dove in, cupping her breasts with both hands before lowering his head and suckling. Her breath ragged, her body bowed, need sharper than she'd ever felt spearing through her, she pushed at his shoulders. The moment he eased back, she undid her jeans, grabbed his hand and thrust it inside her panties.

His eyes dark with desire, he spoke against her lips. "You're so fucking wet for me."

"So fuck me."

He pushed her back on the cool marble island and worked off her jeans and panties. She immediately sat up, yanking his jeans and boxer briefs down. She reached for him and he pulled back.

"One minute," he said through his teeth.

"Hopefully more than that," she purred. She reached for him again, but he remained frustratingly out of reach.

He snagged his jeans from the floor, pulled a condom from his wallet, and ripped it open.

She had a moment—a very brief moment—of self-recrimination for forgetting the condom, but watching him roll it on, thick and ready, the throbbing between her legs intensified. Sharp need trounced everything. "I can't wait to feel you inside me," she told him.

He grunted, finally sheathed himself, then grabbed her, their mouths slamming together as he lifted her partway off the island and thrust fully inside. She broke the kiss, desperate for air. His eyes were hot on hers, his entire body tense as he held himself in check. She didn't want that. She wanted wild. She wrapped her legs around him and kissed him hard. He got the message, thrusting fast and hard and deep. She threw her head back, panting, the tension inside her coiling higher and higher. Hot and hard and unbelievably good.

His voice gravelly, he urged her on. "Come with me."

"You go ahead," she gasped out.

"With me," he bit out.

She closed her eyes, knowing he asked the impossible, there was very little chance of—

He lifted her off him and set her back on her feet. Before she could protest, he turned her around and bent her over the island, taking her in one quick thrust. His body covered hers, his breath hot by her ear. "Let me know what you like, sexy thing."

She felt herself flush at his new nickname for her. He thrust slow and deep, lifting her off the island just enough to cup her breasts with both hands.

"I bet you're luscious everywhere," he murmured.

"Faster," she said. She liked wild, no time for talking.

He pinched her nipple tightly, making her gasp as his other hand slid between her legs, his fingers moving in soft controlled circles. The contrast of rough and gentle made her brain shut down as raw sensations took over. His fingers released their tight hold, massaging her breast, moving to the other breast, rolling and tugging her nipple. A soft moan escaped her lips.

"That's it," he crooned in her ear, "keep talking to me." His teeth scraped the side of her neck before he thrust again, harder this time.

Her head dropped as she surrendered to the pleasure he gave, understanding he wanted to please her.

"Yes," he murmured. "Now you're with me."

He pinched her nipple and she moaned again. He surged within her, filling her more, bringing a delicious ache. He continued playing with her nipple, her insides tightening in response, her moans louder now as his fingers between her legs became more demanding, stroking faster and faster until her entire body trembled, tightening around him. Too much, she thought desperately. White-hot sensations arced through her as he thrust over and over and over, his fingers rocking her, rushing pleasure flooding her body in a tidal wave. A harsh cry ripped from her throat, his deep voice urging her on.

She came hard, ears ringing, heart thundering, her entire body shuddering with the intensity.

"Fuck yes," he growled, grabbing her hips, pounding into her, bringing aftershocks of pleasure so intense she felt it building again, the tension of another release just out of reach. His hand slipped around, pressing firmly against her with each thrust. The sounds she made were primal, sounds she'd never made in her life, and his response was immediate, amping up the intensity, pushing her for more and more. The orgasm shattered her, an explosion of pleasure radiating through her body all the way down to her toes, leaving her shaky and weak. He pulled her tight against him, surging into her for his own release with a guttural sound of male satisfaction.

She tried to catch her breath as he loosened his hold on her hips. She rested against the cool island, soothing her over-heated body, shaky and stunned. He was still inside her, covering her with his body to press a kiss to her shoulder. She sighed.

A moment later, he eased himself off her and pulled out, saying, "Be right back." Probably to get rid of the condom.

She straightened and turned, leaning against the island, working on pulling herself together. She didn't want him to take advantage of her shaky state. Her limbs were heavy, her defenses down, raw and vulnerable. She didn't trust her legs yet.

When she finally felt up to retrieving her scattered clothes, he returned, surprising her yet again. He strode directly to her, no hesitation, still naked, and immediately pulled her into his arms, enveloping her in pure radiant love. His hugs were unlike anything she'd ever felt before. She relaxed, the shaky feeling gone. She wanted to stay like that forever. A trickle of anxiety crept in at the thought.

He spoke, his voice a deep rumble through his chest. "Holy crap!"

She laughed. "Holy crap is right."

Later that night, after eating some leftover turkey-day stuff and not managing to keep his hands off Missy despite both of them being fully dressed, they mutually agreed to take it upstairs. Round one in the kitchen had been fast and furious, inevitable after all their pent-up sexual tension, but Ben planned on taking his time this next go-round.

Nope.

The minute they stepped into his bedroom, they slammed together, mouths hungry, hands grabbing, ripping each other's clothes off. They fell into bed, or maybe he pushed her or she pulled him. It was all a frantic hot blur. He had to get control or he wouldn't last long enough to get her off.

He lifted his head, already panting, half on top of her. "No rushing this time."

"Fuck me."

He swept his thumb over her plump lower lip. The mouth on her, so brazen, so sexy. What had she said before? She spoke all men's language? Like she always wanted mindless fucking, fast and hard. Did she really get off that way? Because it seemed like it had taken some extra-special Ben treatment to get her there before. He kissed her, and she grabbed his ass, pulling him close, her legs spreading for him. His heartbeat roared in his ears. He'd never wanted with this intensity, dangerously close to mindlessly pounding into her. That wasn't him. He always wanted to make sure it was mutual pleasure.

He pulled her grabbing hands from him and pinned them over her head, taking control.

"Let go!" she hollered at the top of her lungs.

He instantly let go, alarmed. "Sorry." Shit. She must've had a bad experience.

She looked away, her voice raw. "I will end this right now and you will be in serious pain."

"My bad. I won't do that again. Promise."

She turned back to him, wary.

"I'm harmless, remember?"

She let out a breath and closed her eyes. "It's a reflex. I'm good. Kiss me again."

He cupped her cheek and kissed her gently. She accepted the kiss, but she wasn't kissing him back like before with wild abandon.

He stroked her hair back from her face. "I want to make you feel good. Will you let me?"

She opened her eyes and nodded.

He brushed his lips over hers, once, twice, coaxing them open before deepening the kiss. She warmed quickly, her fingers running through his hair, kissing him back. He did that for a long while until he was sure she was feeling better about him. Then he placed soft kisses on her temple, her nose, her cheeks, her jaw, watching her relax. He whispered near her ear, "I'm going to kiss and taste every inch of your sexy body, and your hands will be free the entire time to do whatever you want." He met her eyes. "Sound good?"

A small smile played over her lips, the sight so welcome he found himself smiling back. Until she said, "Sounds boring."

He dropped his jaw, feigning offense. "I'll show you boring."

He tickled her and she shrieked, wiggling like crazy, and then he hugged her until she let out a soft sigh. That was the signal he needed, so he went for it, stroking and licking every inch of her, loving the feel of her softness, breathing in her flowery scent, tasting a sexy woman on the verge of wild abandon with every moan, every shiver, every time her fingers ran through his hair. He knew he had her when she started grabbing at his shoulders, trying to pull him in.

"Not done yet," he told her, letting his tongue take another lap around her nipple. "You'll have to wait."

That was when she started the dirty talk and touching herself. She was a temptress, her voice dripping sex, making his cock so fucking hard as she told him how much she wanted him inside her, how hot and wet she was for him, how hard she was going to ride him.

Sheer willpower had him finishing his exploration before he practically dove between her legs, his mouth seeking her out, needing her to get off before his control snapped. He made her tremble, then got her to full-throated glorious feminine bliss, her entire body shuddering with a hard climax. Only then did he fuck her. Or she fucked him. It was hard to tell.

He started out on top. Then she flipped him over with some ninja wrestling move that nearly ended the whole night right there, her knee dangerously close to unmanning him. Luckily he had fast reflexes. "Tell me when you want to change positions," he barked.

"I want to change positions," she barked back.

Then she was on top. Then they rolled, sort of wrestle fucking, and he was on top when she suddenly declared she couldn't come that way.

"I can make you come in any position," he informed her with utmost confidence. He knew women, and he was fast getting to know this woman in particular.

To which she replied, "Sitting up."

So he sat up, she climbed on his lap, and then somehow he was flat on his back, Missy on top again, riding him hard. The moment she tightened around him, he let go, the power of his release roaring through him, heart thundering, breath harsh. Mind-blowingly awesome.

He tried to catch his breath, feeling like he'd been through a hard-core wrestling match where they both won. It was unlike any roll in the sheets he'd ever had, and he couldn't help wondering what the next time would be like. Shit. There wouldn't be a next time. One night, no sleeping over. His euphoria dimmed a bit. He focused on the fact that Missy was the kind of woman who didn't require the hassle of spending the night, which was a relief. How the hell anyone got any sleep all tangled up with another person, he still hadn't figured out. Plus he'd have to share stuff, the bathroom for one, his personal sleeping space for another. He'd have to work around her for his morning routine. The only exception he made was if he sensed the woman needed that post-sex hold-me-forever time. Then he'd make the necessary accommodations. He always wanted the woman to leave his bed feeling good.

She lifted off him and flopped on the mattress next to him.

A pang of loss went through him the moment her body left his. Obviously, his stupid libido wanted more wild sex. Not now but soon. He told himself to appreciate what they had. He took a deep breath in and out. Fuck it, he was too spent to worry about it. All he wanted to do was sleep.

He glanced over at her. She was staring at the ceiling, eyes wide open next to him. Was she waiting for him to invite her to spend the night? He'd thought they'd agreed not to do that.

He stared at the ceiling too, purposely not drawing the blanket over them, waiting to see if she settled in with the blanket or rolled out of bed and got dressed. He looked over at her.

She turned her head and gave him a tight smile.

They both stared at the ceiling. Awkward.

Long minutes ticked by, his skin cooling. The urge to pull the blanket on intensified, but he'd be damned if he was the reason she spent the night. He'd wait her out.

She cleared her throat.

"Yeah?" he asked.

"Nothing. Just had a tickle in my throat."

"You cold?" *Maybe want a blanket or to get dressed?*

"I'm fine. You?"

"I'm good." *Cold but good.*

Damn, this woman played a mean game of chicken. She

made no move to stay or go, and he couldn't read her. Maybe it wouldn't be so bad if she stayed. They could have more wild sex in the morning. So what if he didn't sleep, right? It would be worth it.

Five minutes later, he offered the invitation, working hard to sound neutral about the whole idea. "Did you, uh, want to spend the night or…"

She sat up. "As much as I appreciate your reluctant invitation—"

"Who said it was reluctant?" Maybe a little vague. He didn't want her to stay, yet he kinda did too.

She narrowed her eyes. "Don't insult my intelligence."

He bit back a smile. "It seemed the thing to do. I didn't know if you were a cuddler—"

"I'm not."

"Cool. Me either."

"We agreed no spending the night," she said with some bite. Her feet hit the floor and she stood. Then she gathered her clothes off the floor and headed to the adjoining bathroom to dress, shutting the door behind her. Like he hadn't just seen, touched, and licked every inch of her. That dressing-in-the-bathroom move, along with her sharp tone, meant he had to smooth things over. He didn't want it to be a big thing when they saw each other again, as they inevitably would with all the friends they had in common. He wanted her to leave here feeling good.

He didn't want her to leave.

He threw an arm over his eyes, tired but wound tight. Now he didn't know what he wanted where Missy was concerned, and she was mad. Wild sex fucked with his thinking.

He pulled the covers up, propped the pillows behind him, and waited. When she finally emerged, fully dressed, he tried to soothe her ruffled feathers. "Hey, sexy thing."

She laughed a little. "That's better than cactus. Thanks for tonight. Sorry about my freak-out."

"No problem. That's on me."

She shook her head. "No, it wasn't you. My ex was bad

news—" she waved that away "—you don't need to hear all that stuff. It's in the past."

Except she was clearly still affected. "I'm a good listener if you want to talk about it." Nonjudgmental listening had been a way of life in his house with his social worker mom. Didn't mean he necessarily wanted to share as a kid, but he always knew he could.

She worried her lower lip. "Thanks, but no. I'd like to just enjoy the afterglow. It was…well, you know, holy crap." She brightened. "I guess that means good."

Good? Just good? How about great? Outstanding! Phenomenal!

"Yup," he said. The sex had been mind-blowing. Wasn't it? She couldn't have faked those full-body shudders. Right?

She slipped on her sneakers. "Happy Thanksgiving."

A chest pang alarmed him because that felt like goodbye forever. "You too," he half growled.

She walked over to him, leaned down, and kissed him. A quick peck, nothing more, then she walked out the door, smiling to herself.

He flopped down on the mattress, staring at the ceiling, trying to figure out what the hell was wrong with him. He should feel relaxed and happy. It wasn't often the chemistry worked that well. He sat up, tossed the extra pillow off the bed, punched his own pillow, then flopped down on his side, staring at the open bedroom door.

She wasn't coming back.

Long moments passed and he got more and more agitated.

He turned off the light on his nightstand and closed his eyes, tossing and turning. Sleep eluded him.

Dammit. Obviously he needed another wild night with her before he could let her go. Now he had to seduce her all over again.

Seriously, how many times did she have to be dropped into his lap for him to get the message? He got it. Fate kept bringing them together. Oh, yeah, he was a believer now. And when fate put a woman like Missy in your path, you welcomed her with open arms until the thing was done. Two, three nights max oughta do it. He hoped. He wasn't looking for serious. He just wanted a little more time with her.

His mind replayed every minute of their naked time, and he got himself even more worked up, both wanting her and agitated at the idea of never having her again. Hell, she'd really gotten under his skin.

Hours later, he gave up on sleep and took a long hot shower, taking himself in hand, imagining her sexy mouth on him.

He leaned against the shower wall, spent, knowing he was going to have to work harder for a woman than he ever had in his life.

6

———

Missy started her new temp job at the Eastman mall the next day with as much quiet dignity as she could muster given her outfit—green velvet dress with a red sash, white tights patterned with giant candy canes, felt shoes curled up at the toes, and a large pointy green hat. Yes, she was an elf.

Think of the children. The Harper family needed her. This was good, honest work at Santa's Workshop. All she had to do was get through the next three weeks and four days and she'd have enough to repay the money Louis had stolen. She'd have to settle for Christmas shopping the sales online now that her free time was taken up with a second shift. Not as satisfying to shop that way, but whatever.

Thankfully, her first day, though hellishly long, had proceeded without incident. More importantly, she hadn't run into anyone she knew. She certainly hadn't told anyone of her new job. She'd never live it down.

Now it was Saturday and she was determined to power through with Christmas cheer intact.

"Yo, new elf," her baby-faced boss said. Chris? Christian? She couldn't remember. Yesterday when he'd introduced himself, all she heard was *click-clack* due to his tongue piercing. "You forgot *click* the jingle bells *clack*."

She put a hand to her chest where the jingle bell necklace

should've been. "Shoot. I'll run and get it." She must've left it back in the mall locker room where she'd changed.

"No time *click*," he said. "We got *clack* a line *clack* already."

She peered around a large candy cane column to find a huge line of kids fidgeting with excitement, waiting for their big moment with the jolly man himself. Their parents were doing their best to keep them presentable in their Christmas card photo-ready best.

"Santa's not here yet," she told her boss. "I'll be quick."

"Santa's arrival is timed for dramatic effect. Hang on." Tongue-clack boy reached into a small storage trunk near the camera stand and emerged with a shiny red nose with red string that looked like it belonged on Pennywise, the terrifying clown from Stephen King's *It*. She suppressed a shudder.

He offered the nose. "Here, you can be Rudolph."

She stared at it in horror. "I'll look like a scary clown. The kids will run away from me."

"You won't look scary. Just tell them you're Rudolph the Red-Nosed Elf."

She was so distraught she couldn't even hear his tongue click-clacking. Rudolph the Red-Nosed Elf or Pennywise the Terrifying Elf? "Isn't there anything else in the trunk?"

He pawed through the small trunk. "Extra granny glasses for Mrs. Claus, white beard for Santa, and somebody left a Santa belly in here." He looked up. "That must've been from the skinny Santa who quit."

"Great."

"You giving me attitude on your second day?" he snapped, straightening to his full height, a mere inch taller than her five feet three. "Just because I'm young doesn't mean I tolerate insubordination."

Ooh, big word. "No attitude," she said, taking the Rudolph nose and not putting it on. Maybe she could wait him out.

"Let's see it."

She gamely put it on. "Merry Christmas," she said with a bright smile. If anyone saw her in this getup, she'd bolt behind the nearest candy cane. She was sure she was somewhere between absolutely ridiculous and terrifying. Either way, her friends would have a field day if they spotted her.

"Perfect. The kids will go nuts."

And boy, did they ever. She was the official greeter at the front of the line, keeping the kids back until it was their turn. Not one kid was put off by the nose. Guess they hadn't discovered Pennywise yet. The little ones rushed her legs, hugging her tight, asking to be picked up so they could beep her nose. She deflected by asking them to sing "Rudolph the Red-Nosed Reindeer" to make Rudolph feel at home at the Eastman mall. It was cute.

Two hours later, feet aching from the pointy shoes, hungry, with the beginnings of a headache from the incessant Christmas carol soundtrack piped into the North Pole and the sounds of children squealing and screaming over Rudolph elf, the cuteness wore off. Big time. Also her nose was sweating. She feared the red might rub off and she'd have to explain to her friends why she was a red-nosed Missy.

A little boy smacked a metal Hot Wheels car into her shin as he rushed at her. *Ow!*

His mom pulled the boy off, but the car caught on her tights, pulling them before breaking free. She looked down, assessing the damage. Great. Now her tights had a hole in them that would surely get bigger as she moved around. At least she wasn't bleeding.

"So sorry," the boy's mom said. She turned to her son. "Tell the nice woman you're sorry."

"Sowwy," the boy said. "Can I beep your nose?"

Missy heroically refrained from covering her nose. "No, but you can sing 'Rudolph the Red-Nosed Reindeer.' Santa loves to hear Christmas cheer."

The boy launched into an off-key Rudolph that made her ears ring.

She stifled a sigh. She'd have to buy another set of tights on her lunch break. Unless they had extras lying around somewhere. She approached Mrs. Claus standing to the side, smiling and waving at the children walking past Santa's Workshop.

"Any chance there's more candy cane tights around here?" Missy asked her.

"They're too cheap to order extras," the woman responded in a rough smoker's voice. "Try the Christmas shop on the second floor."

Okay, she'd take the elevator not far from here, book it to the shop, book it to the locker room, and be back before any random Christmas shopper could recognize her.

Her boss appeared again, hands behind his back, all business as he did a tour of Santa's Workshop, checking on the merry situation. He took one look at her and rushed over. "You're on break. Fix the tights situation, preferably with a candy cane pattern. Rudolph would also be good." He pulled out his wallet and handed her a twenty-dollar bill. "I'll deduct it from your paycheck."

"Thanks," she bit out. She took off the awful nose, then the pointy hat, tucking the nose inside. She went to set it on the shelf behind the photo counter when he stopped her.

"What do you think you're doing?" he demanded. "Keep the hat on your person at all times. You know how many kids would love to play with this? And I can tell you right now elf hats don't come cheap."

"Okay, okay." She tucked the hat under her arm and quickly skirted the crowd of kids, slipping around a candy cane column, the glass elevator in the center of the mall within sight. The elevator was packed, so she figured she'd squeeze into the middle for maximum camouflage. The escalator was too risky—a long walk away and she'd be in plain view of any and all curious shoppers.

She hurried as fast as she could in pointy elf shoes, feeling decidedly more duck-like than she wanted to think about, and hit the elevator button. *Come on, come on.*

"Missy Higgins, this must be fate!"

No-o-o-o!

~

Ben didn't bother to keep the laughter from his voice. "You know," he drawled, "I've always had this secret elf fantasy. Maybe we should see what happens."

Missy the elf turned, scratching her bright pink cheek with her middle finger.

He barked out a laugh. It had been two days since their hookup, and he'd planned on calling her today to see if she wanted to grab a bite to eat. He'd missed her, not just the sex. She was funny and smart, a tough woman who gave as good as she got, which made her easy to be around. He could relax with her, no bending over backwards to avoid hurting sensitive feelings. And he'd never met anyone who, like him, was adopted as a baby and orphaned a second time. That seemed special, a unique common reference. Plus fate made them keep running into each other. Now he just had to charm the elf panties off her. Did elves wear panties?

He gave her an appreciative once-over. She was a sight. The green velvet dress with fake white fur along the edges and a red sash around her small waist were sexy if you were into the elf look, which he definitely was now that it was on her. Nice and snug too with a short fluffy skirt.

Her eyes flashed. "Shut up."

A small laugh escaped. "I didn't say anything."

A few more people joined them, waiting for the elevator, an elderly man and a mom pushing a toddler in a stroller. No one could keep their eyes off Missy. She stared straight ahead, her cheeks and neck pink.

The elevator doors opened, and a pile of strollers rolled out, parents behind them. He let everyone go in ahead of him and then followed Missy inside.

"Where ya headed?" he asked.

"To the Christmas store."

"To the Christmas store!" he exclaimed. "Is that where the mall elves go to build toys?"

The elderly gentleman laughed quietly. The toddler in the stroller stared up at Missy in awe.

"Yes," she said through her teeth. Her cheeks dotted with red on top of the pink; even her nose was red. Clearly she was embarrassed to be caught elfing on the side. He should play nice.

Naughty was his middle name.

"Why is your nose red?" he asked. "I've never seen anyone blush like that."

"I don't want to talk about it," she bit out.

Silence fell, everyone in the elevator discreetly checking out the disgruntled elf, him included.

The elevator doors opened and they stepped out. He kept stride with Missy doing her best to motor through the mall in those ridiculous curly-toed shoes.

"Why don't you try it without the shoes?" he asked.

She stopped and narrowed her eyes. "I'm trying to hurry. I have to buy tights, change, eat lunch, and be back in under an hour. In case you haven't noticed, the mall is packed, and there's sure to be a line at the Christmas store. I might even have to go to more than one store if they don't have what I need."

He held out his hand. "Shoe."

She grabbed his arm for balance, taking one off. "Fine." She took the other one off and held them both in one hand. "What're you doing here? I thought you did your Christmas shopping at the craft bazaar."

"That was Grandmom's Christmas shopping."

She continued speed walking, much faster without the shoes. "So you're willing to brave the mall for…"

"Watch battery."

"That's too bad. Shoulda got it online."

"It was a grandmom emergency." Besides, the mall had a watch battery kiosk and was close to his house.

Missy smiled for some reason like maybe he'd been suckered.

It had been odd now that he thought about it. His grandmother had made a huge fuss over the watch not keeping the correct time, saying she felt "disoriented" and kept showing up places late, though she'd shown up at his place exactly on time this morning for breakfast. She liked to check on him on a weekly basis to make sure he wasn't letting his house "go to pot." Whatever that meant. He had a cleaning service. She'd had a weird dream too about him marrying a redhead. She often had bizarre dreams that he never thought twice about, but now that he was looking at the brunette he knew to be a redhead, he was beginning to get suspicious. This was the second errand he'd run for his grandmother where he also ran into Missy. Was Missy friendly with his grandmother? They did go to the same church, though his grandmother had a different last name than him, so Missy might not have known they were related.

He was about to ask when Missy suddenly slipped, hat and shoes flying, landing on her ass. She swore a blue streak.

He gathered her stuff for her. "Are you hurt?"

"Just my pride."

He grinned. "Is that what you call your ass?"

She glared at him.

He tried really hard to dial down his smile. "Funny how we both fell on our asses in front of each other. You might say we're falling for each other." He winked and offered his hand to help her up.

She ignored his hand and slowly got to her feet. She took her hat and shoes back. "Don't you have a watch battery to buy?"

He patted his jeans pocket. "Right here. I was about to head out when I caught sight of your elfishness."

"Laugh it up." She walked at a more sedate pace, probably a little sore from her fall.

He instantly felt remorse. "I'm sorry, I was being insensitive to your elf situation. Elves have feelings too. Here, let me hold your elf hat and elf shoes."

"Could you say elf one more time?" She handed them over, seeming glad to be rid of them.

"Elf."

She narrowed her eyes, the effect still adorable with her little green elf dress.

He bit back a laugh. "What? You asked. Let me buy you lunch to make up for all of my elf insensitivity."

She gave him side eye. "You don't have to do that. And I'd

really appreciate it if you didn't tell anyone what you saw here today."

"My lips are sealed."

When they arrived at the Christmas store, she took her hat and shoes back. "So, um, bye. Please wipe your memory of this entire embarrassing time."

"I'm not embarrassed at all."

She threw her hands up.

He grinned. "What're you buying?"

"Candy cane tights or Rudolph. My stupid tights have a hole."

He'd noticed but refrained from commenting what with all the other great stuff she had going on. "I thought you were doing a goth elf look."

She cracked a smile. "I need something that goes with this." She held open the hat to show him a red Rudolph nose. He pressed his lips into a flat line. Good thing he hadn't seen her wearing that too or he wouldn't have been able to stop laughing.

She whirled and went into the store. He took a deep breath and followed into the ninth circle of hell. The music was deafening, something about a Christmas donkey, bright lights flashing on Christmas trees dazzled the eyes in the worst way, and a giant inflatable snowman with a clear belly full of snowmen bizarrely took center stage.

He stopped behind her at the novelty socks and tights section. "What size are you?"

She startled. "Geez, Ben, make some noise before you sneak up on someone."

"I'm not exactly stealth. You were just lost in the beauty of…are these mistletoe tights? Hell yeah. I'll meet you under there."

"Under where?" she asked absently.

He chuckled.

"How old are you again?" She grabbed a pair of white tights with little Christmas trees. "Close enough."

"I'm thirty-one going down on…how old are you?"

She pursed her lips, trying not to smile, her eyes dancing with amusement before she headed toward the register.

He followed. "Yeah, don't worry about the mistletoe tights. I have a good feeling about those elf panties."

She shot him a dark look. "Shh."

He gave her his dimpled elf-panty-melting smile.

She shook her head, laughing as she took her place at the end of a long line.

"What do you want for lunch?" he asked. "I'll get it while you change your tights."

She turned to him, a light of surprise in her eyes. "That would actually be really helpful. I usually pack a lunch, but I didn't have the energy to grocery shop last night."

"See, I can be thoughtful, considerate…" He paused, trying to think up more good stuff women liked, when she finished for him.

"Don't forget modest. Can you get me a taco salad at the Mexican place in the food court?"

"*Sí, sí, senorita.* On me, okay?"

She nodded and smiled. "*Gracias.*"

"Give me your phone. I'll put my number in so you can text me when you get to the food court."

She pulled it from a side pocket in her skirt and handed it over. Now this was progress. He entered his number and handed it back. "See ya soon."

She shifted forward in line. "See ya."

Twenty minutes later, his phone vibrated with a text from Missy. *All set.*

Just about to pay. Where are you?

Sitting across from Yo-Fro.

He turned, scanning the crowded space, and spotted her. She looked worn out, head resting in her hand. Guilt stabbed at him. Here she was working hard on a second shift and he'd been not-so-secretly laughing at her.

He strode over to her table, setting her lunch in front of her, and took the seat directly across from her. She immediately dug in like she was starving.

After a couple of bites, she stopped and looked up at him. "Aren't you going to eat?"

"I'm still full from breakfast. Omelet with the works. My specialty breakfast. Maybe one day you'll get to experience it yourself."

She spoke around a mouthful of salad. "Let's not pretend you wanted me to spend the night."

He leaned forward. "I was going to call you."

She took another bite, chewed and swallowed. "I didn't give you my number."

"I looked you up. I can find most anything on the internet."

Her brows drew together, but she didn't comment.

"But then I ran into you. Missy—" he took a deep breath "—I don't think we're done."

She opened her bottled water and took a long drink.

"You want to grab dinner tonight?" he asked.

She put the water bottle down. "Can't. Got plans."

"What kind of plans?"

"The kind with my friends," she said evenly.

"What about after?"

She took another forkful of salad. "For a booty call? No, thanks."

His neck burned. He did make it sound like that. So much for charm. "What about Sunday for a date?"

"Working." She put her fork down. "Look, Ben, we agreed to one night. I don't understand what you want from me."

He wanted more time with her. "What's one more time? We keep running into each other anyway."

"I'm sorry, I just—"

He held up a hand. "Nope, no need to be sorry. I got it."

She smiled. "Thanks. And thanks for lunch too. I appreciate your help today."

He'd never been in this position before, trying to extend the hookup to more. Usually women wanted more from him, not the other way around. Was he just drawn to the chase?

Irritated to be so off his game, he shut his mouth. She continued eating, completely focused on her salad.

Finally, he had to ask, "Why're you working as an elf?"

She glanced up at him, cheeks pink. "I thought I told you this before. Just picking up a little extra cash for the holidays."

"For presents?"

"Yes."

He studied her for a minute. It seemed like this was a tough gig just to buy a few extra presents. He leaned close. "Why're you really doing it? I can't imagine you enjoy being an elf."

She sighed. "I have a good reason."

"Which is?"

She was quiet, setting her fork down like she'd lost her appetite.

Every instinct in him told him something serious was going on with Missy. She was clearly a woman in need. And he always came through for a woman in need. He'd spent half his life caring for his sick mom—she'd suffered from terrible migraines from the brain cancer—and he'd been more parent than kid sometimes. She'd called him Super Ben because he always came to the rescue. It was a part of him that he couldn't turn off.

He got serious. "Missy, you can tell me. I won't tell a soul."

She worried her lower lip for a moment. "I was raising money for a family in need for Christmas. That's what the craft bazaar was about. Everyone donated most of their profits, and then someone stole the money. More than two thousand dollars. I'm trying to earn it back."

"Did you report it stolen?"

"No. I didn't want anyone to know after all the work they put in to make the bazaar a success. I figured I'd just quietly replace the money. I'm the one who was collecting the money anyway, and I'm the one doing all the Christmas shopping for the family."

He stared at her, an unexpected lump in his throat. She took this ridiculous elf job to help a family in need? She wasn't just a tough woman, underneath all that, she cared deeply about others. That meant a lot to him, a value he'd been raised with that he took to heart. "Missy, I'll give you the money—"

"No. It's my problem. I'll fix it."

He blew out a breath. "Why is it your problem? It's not like *you* stole the money."

"It just is. Now drop it." She broke off a piece of the taco salad bowl and chomped it ferociously. She was just being stubborn.

Don't do it. Don't you offer her that admin job.

It would be *hell*, knowing how much he wanted her, knowing how good it could be, knowing how much he liked her and wanted to spend more time with her, only to keep a line of professionalism between them. He could *not* have her in his office day in, day out and deny all of his natural instincts.

She stood abruptly, grabbed her elf shoes, and hung onto the back of her chair, slipping them on. "I'd better get back to work. Thanks for lunch."

"I'm heading out." He crossed to her side and took her tray from the table. "I'll escort you to the North Pole so you don't get accosted by some eager kids."

"I'm more afraid of getting accosted by you."

That stung. "Seriously?"

She smiled and squeezed his arm. "Kidding. You've been very helpful."

"It's kinda my thing." He dumped the trash, and they took the escalator at the end of the food court back down to Santa's Workshop.

She turned to him. "You know what's great about being an elf with a Rudolph nose?"

He smiled. "What?"

"Spreading Christmas cheer," she said deadpan.

They cracked up.

"Seriously, though, it's worth it," she said, "though I confess my first thought was Pennywise. You know that terrifying clown from *It*?"

He laughed. "I don't think you could ever pull off terrifying in that dress."

"I guess not. The kids were thrilled. Anyway, I can't wait to make Christmas special for the Harper kids. There's three of them, and I think the two youngest might still believe in Santa. They've been through so much, and I just want their first Christmas in their new home to be perfect."

His chest ached with all her heartfelt sentiment. "You're a good person, Missy Higgins."

She blushed. "It's not me. A lot of people helped."

"Just say thank you."

"I'm not good with compliments."

He waggled his brows. "How's this for a compliment? You make a beautiful—" he leaned close to her ear "—dare I say, sexy elf."

She snort-laughed. "I'm going to get a big head, and then how would it fit in my pointy hat?"

"You know what you need? Some elf ears."

"Don't even mention it. My boss would be all over that."

"Maybe some jingle bells—"

"I'm already in trouble for forgetting my jingle bell necklace. Shit. I forgot it again. I was just in the locker room. I was in such a rush, I didn't even think about it."

"I'm sure it's fine."

They got off the escalator, heading for Santa's Workshop, Missy telling him all about her baby-faced boss with a click-clacking tongue and then doing a hysterical impersonation of him. "Keep the hat on your person at all times!" she bellowed. "I can tell you right now elf hats don't come cheap!"

"I'm glad you found that funny," a voice snapped.

They both turned to find a short red-faced man, couldn't have been more than twenty, practically frothing at the mouth. "You're fired."

"What?" Missy exclaimed. "I'm sorry, that was in poor taste. It won't happen again."

The man remained stone-faced. "Security will escort you

to the locker room. I want all of that costume, including the jingle bell necklace."

The distraught look on Missy's face had Ben stepping in. "She said she was sorry. We were just joking around."

"Tell it to security." The little weasel waved a security guard over. The security guard, a bald man with a huge beer belly, hopped to it, looking happy to have something to do.

"It was my fault," Ben said. "I did my boss impression, so she did hers."

Missy shot him a look that said *really?* He lifted one shoulder. It was hard to deny what had happened when the guy had heard everything.

Missy turned to her boss as the security guard stepped close to her side. "I'm not a flight risk, you moron," she snapped. "Here." She shoved the hat and Rudolph nose into the guy's hands. Then she took off her shoes and threw them at him.

"Hey!" The guy ducked. "She accosted me! Did you see that?"

"Why don't you try being an elf?" Missy spat. "You already look like a troll."

She turned on her heel and stalked off, the security guard quickly joining her.

Ben didn't have to think twice. He turned and followed her. Fucking A, he was going to offer her that admin job.

7

Missy emerged from the mall locker room in her wool coat, sweater, and jeans, elf costume in hand, still pissed not only to be fired but that her boss actually called for security. What woman in their right mind would be caught dead wearing this elf getup anywhere but here?

She stepped through the employees-only door out to the mall, where the security guard regarded her with a stern expression. She handed over the costume without a word. The guy marched off importantly.

She turned and spotted Ben leaning on the wall near the exit. He lifted a hand, apparently waiting for her. She waved back. Now that she wasn't humiliatingly dressed as an elf, giving him way too much ammunition, she took a moment to appreciate the big and bad vibe he had going on. His short-cropped hair, the sharp lines of his cheekbones and jaw, his large muscular body framed perfectly in his black leather jacket and faded jeans—all of it combined made him look tough and sexy. She liked the contrast in his looks with his thoughtful considerate manner. She'd never met another man like him.

Sure, he didn't hesitate to tease her, but he could be serious when the occasion called for it. Like when she'd freaked when he'd restrained her wrists in bed. Her ex, Louis, would do that, manacle her wrists in one hand above her head and slap her. He never left a bruise, just let her know when he was mad for any tiny infraction, imagined or otherwise. He'd be so sorry afterward, lavishing her with gifts and attention for weeks, promising it'd never happen again. She'd married him at eighteen, scared and alone, and he'd promised to take care of her. Their first year of marriage had been good and then two years of abuse. It had happened so gradually, a slap here and there, grabbing her by the hair, the yelling. She'd finally faced facts and told him she wanted a divorce. He'd nearly strangled her, saying he'd kill her before he let her go. She'd been lucky to escape, managing to reach the bedside lamp and knock him out.

Her boss, Amy, had helped Missy get out of California and settled with a new job in a new city, Seattle. Amy was also the one that helped Missy get a lawyer and file for divorce. Missy sent money back to Amy whenever she could to pay back the lawyer's fees. Life went on, Missy a lot smarter about men. Love wasn't worth the risk. No man would ever have that power over her again.

She headed toward Ben. He straightened out of his slouch and met her halfway, stopping in front of her.

"That's the first time I've been fired in my life." She threw up her hands. "From an elf job!"

He spoke in a deadly serious tone. "You need a job; I have a job. Come work for me and Logan. We could use an admin. Ours is out until after the New Year. Her daughter just had her first baby and she went up to Vermont to be with her."

"Work for you?" she echoed, shocked at the offer. Ben in a position of authority over her? Ben tempting her at the office? Ben, Ben, Ben, every day for the next three weeks and change? That sounded like trouble. He'd want to be on top in more ways than one. "Ben, I do appreciate—"

He cut her off. "I know you're trying to do something really special for this family, and I get that you want to earn your own way. If you want to pick up some admin work for Checkin, the job is yours. It's just me and Logan at the office, quiet for the most part. We're not the hovering kind of bosses.

And Sabrina works in the same building, so you could meet up with her for lunch or whatever."

Her firm resolve to turn him down wavered. That did sound nice. Sabrina was a good friend of hers, living in the apartment down the hall, one of her first friends when she'd moved to Clover Park. And Ben wouldn't really be her boss, she reasoned. She'd just be helping him and Logan out for a few weeks. Logan, the youngest son in the Campbell clan, was a sweetheart, easygoing and mellow. He'd be no trouble at all. Plus it would be so much easier to be back at a desk than dealing with seasonal work at the mall. Her next (only) idea had been to work at a retail store that needed extra help, probably also at the crowded mall.

She decided it could work if they were both professionals. "I've been an admin for eleven years, executive assistant for six of them, and I'm comfortable with most office applications, including spreadsheets and databases. I work in construction now, but I used to work at a tech company in Seattle."

"That's perfect because we are a tech company. Logan is the tech guy, actually. I'm more the numbers guy."

She nodded. "I work mornings at Marino and Capello Construction through the end of the year. Things are slow for them this time of year. Would afternoons work for you?"

He looked at a point over her shoulder. "Sure. This would only be through Christmas Eve. We're shutting down for the holidays."

His tone was so flat, so distant, she got worried. "Are you sure you want me to take this job?"

He finally met her eyes, his expression downright gloomy. "Yes, I'm sure."

"Because you need my skills?" she asked, feeling him out. She wasn't used to this somber version of Ben. Something felt off.

He exhaled sharply. "Because you need a job."

She stared at him. "That's it?"

His lips pressed flatly together before he spoke in a nearly robotic voice. "And I need an admin."

She crossed her arms. "As long as we keep it strictly professional."

"Of course," he snapped. "Did you doubt I would be anything but professional?"

She uncrossed her arms, taken aback by his hostile tone. "I didn't mean to imply…I'm sorry. Really. I guess I thought because of before—" She stopped herself, deciding it was better not to mention their hookup in light of their new professional relationship. "Thank you and I accept your offer."

"Spit oath." He pretended to spit in his hand, a hint of amusement back in his eyes. "Total professionals."

She relaxed, so relieved he was back to his usual self. She pretend spit and shook his hand.

"Eww." He dropped her hand. "Slimy. You weren't really supposed to spit."

She laughed, a huge weight lifting off her shoulders. She'd come through for the Harpers. And Ben would be fun to be around. As long as they kept a little distance between them at the office, neither one of them would be tempted. And Logan would be there too, so it wasn't like Ben would be stealing kisses in front of his business partner. This would be good.

She headed toward the exit, already planning ahead to the errands she'd run with her suddenly free afternoon, grocery shopping at the top of the list.

Ben kept pace with her. "You want something in writing? An official professional contract?"

"I don't need it in writing. I'll take your word."

"Good, my word is gold."

"I'm sure."

He stopped short. "I'm serious. I won't break my word to you. Ever. Especially when it comes to business. I'll treat you like any other employee."

He was saying all the right things, but part of her felt let down. Kind of disappointing after all their, um, chemistry. "Thanks, Ben. I'm looking forward to it."

"See ya Monday," he said brusquely and strode toward the exit.

She watched him go, admiring his rear view with just a hint of a swagger, and sighed. Why did she want him even more now that he'd sworn to be professional? It was just such an upright gentlemanly thing to do to put her at ease, even knowing she was just a temp.

The man was worse than trouble. He was irresistible.

~

After the eleven a.m. Mass the next morning, Missy exited the church and met up with the supersweet Mrs. Walsh, waving and smiling at her from the sidewalk. She wore a glaringly bright fuchsia puffy down coat with a matching fuchsia knitted cap over her wispy jaw-length white hair.

Missy put a hand on Mrs. Walsh's arm. "Are you sure you should be out in this weather?" It was cold enough to snow, and she'd said she was coming down with something last week.

Mrs. Walsh's breath came out in a cold puff of air. "I'm okay. I heard the craft bazaar was a huge success. Congratulations!"

Her gut twisted, shame over the stolen money nearly making her lose her smile, but Missy toughed it out. "Thanks, it was. Everyone worked really hard to pull it together."

"Don't be so modest. We all know you were the dynamo who made it happen."

"It was definitely a group effort."

"Bah. So, what's new?"

Missy's attention caught on the Harper family descending the stairs of the church. Rena, a petite brunette with long hair, struggled to get her two rambunctious sons, Todd and Will, to walk not run. Their older sister, Madelyn, ten years old and wearing a pink jacket a size too small, ducked her head and followed her family out. A weight pressed on Missy's chest. She remembered vividly what it felt like to be ten years old with clothes that didn't fit because no one had the money for more, and worse, to have your whole world turned upside down. That would be the first Christmas present she bought, a new winter coat for Madelyn. A small comfort, but sometimes the little things could mean the world to a child.

"Good morning, Rena," Mrs. Walsh called. "Morning to you too, Todd, Will, and Madelyn."

"How are you?" Missy called.

The boys were too busy shoving each other to notice the greeting.

"Hi," Madelyn said softly, shoving her hands in her jacket pockets and staring at the ground.

"Morning," Rena said, scooping a glove that had just fallen out of one of the boys' pockets off the sidewalk. "Sorry, no time this morning. Got to get to the supermarket before the snowstorm hits."

"Snow!" the boys shouted.

"I could go for you," Missy said.

"That's okay," Rena said, shooing the boys down the sidewalk. "It's part of an economics lesson for the kids too."

They hurried off. Missy turned to Mrs. Walsh. "Is she homeschooling them?"

"No, they're enrolled at Clover Park Elementary. I think she's teaching them life lessons. Got to learn them some day, might as well when they're young."

"I guess."

"Anything new with you?" Mrs. Walsh smiled, her brown eyes twinkling like she knew something. Had Mrs. Walsh spotted her at the mall in her elf costume?

Missy fought the heat creeping up her neck. "Can't think of anything."

"No-o-o?" Mrs. Walsh sang. "Maybe a new job, new fella, that sort of thing."

Missy focused on the non-elf part. "Fella?"

"You know, a boyfriend. How do you young people say it now? A hookup?"

Missy sucked in air. Were people at church gossiping about the Missy-Ben make-out session at the craft bazaar last weekend?

"Did you hear something about me?" Missy asked.

Mrs. Walsh smiled serenely. "No, I just noticed you have a little glow about you like maybe some good news happened."

A glow? Did she still have a glow from hooking up with Ben three days ago? Or, the more likely scenario, Ben was telling people they'd hooked up. Gossip spread fast in this town. How crass. And here she'd thought he might be the kind of guy who could keep a confidence. This was just great. Next thing you knew he'd be blabbing to everyone about her humiliating time as an elf. She'd be known as Missy the slutty elf.

"Nope," Missy lied. "No news here. How about you?"

Mrs. Walsh gave Missy's hand a squeeze. "I'm hoping for some good news soon. I wish the same for you."

"Thanks," Missy said.

"I've been praying for you," Mrs. Walsh said.

Missy cocked her head. "Why…" She trailed off because Mrs. Walsh was already halfway down the sidewalk, spry for a woman in her eighties.

Mrs. Walsh lifted a hand, calling over her shoulder. "My prayers will be answered soon! I have a good feeling."

Missy stared at the woman's retreating back, her fuchsia coat floating out around her like a giant candy cloud. The woman meant well, but sometimes she just made no sense.

8

Ben couldn't concentrate Monday morning, knowing Missy would be showing up at one o'clock today. There was work to be done, of course. He and Logan had to keep up with their current clients, figure out marketing for after the holidays to bring in new clients, and they were also setting up investor meetings for January. Checkin was valued at 250 million, and they were looking to raise forty million more to expand with a sales force and even better tech that integrated with some of the older HR systems. They were on the verge, an exciting time for them. Logan's big brother Jake owned a very successful tech company and had the connections they needed with Silicon Valley investors. Jake hadn't offered to fund them and they hadn't asked. Mostly because they didn't want to muck up family and money. All the guys knew if they asked wealthy Jake for funds for just about anything, he'd step up, but Ben and Logan didn't want to take the easy way out. This company was all theirs, and they wanted to do it on their own. Kinda like Missy wanting to earn the money on her own to help that family. Another thing they had in common.

Fate.

Get your head on straight!

He drummed his fingers on his desk. His plan was simple

—spend these three weeks and two days getting to know Missy as a professional and treating her like a valued employee. The last thing he needed was another disgruntled employee like Ashley. He could not fail. The stakes were too high with the upcoming investor meetings. They couldn't afford another black mark against him, and he never wanted to let Logan down.

Sex was *off* the table.

No, it was more than off the table, he would take a vow of celibacy. He shifted uncomfortably. Maybe he should find an outlet for all this pent-up lust. If only he wasn't so hooked on Missy. Never had a hookup gotten under his skin like she did. Maybe getting to know each other with no sex would lead to some deeper level. Or not. He wasn't sure how deep he was willing to go in. He wasn't much for relationships, but this thing with Missy felt different. Hell, maybe they'd end up hating each other after this. Maybe she only wanted sex from him. He could only guess what was going on in her mind. She was practically a closed book.

He had to know more.

He found himself clicking over to the Checkin website, logging in, and entering Missy's name. Since he couldn't stop thinking about her, might as well find out more. It wasn't like he wouldn't do the same for any temp employee. That was the whole point of Checkin—background checks for short-term employees. Though more and more companies were taking an interest for all new hires. He'd already Googled Missy after they'd hooked up and hadn't found much on her, just the basics—phone number and address. Bingo. She'd been married before to Louis Braxton, divorced three years later. Geez, she'd been young when she got married, right out of high school. Maybe she'd been pregnant. Maybe she had kids. Maybe the money she was trying to earn for the holidays was for her own family. What was her deal?

She was thirty, a year younger than him. No criminal record. Clean driving record. Several name changes—Carson, Higgins, Braxton, Higgins. Maybe Carson was her name before she was adopted. He wanted to know more.

A hand slapped down on his desk, making him jump. "I want those reports by five p.m. sharp!"

He met Logan's very amused brown eyes, his own cheeks burning from being caught snooping. "Asshole. When ya gonna shave, huh?" Logan sported a neatly trimmed light brown beard and mustache, going all hipster on him. He took after his blonde beauty queen mom, the only Campbell brother with light brown hair, the rest of them had dark brown, and he had her narrow nose that tilted up at the end like a ski jump. A pretty boy jock—his features too perfect— turned techie hipster. Women loved to gaze upon Logan, but he was never serious with anyone, still stuck on his college girlfriend. The one who got away.

"You look guilty as hell." Logan rushed behind Ben's desk to peer over his shoulder. "Whatcha looking at? Porn?"

Ben slammed his laptop shut. "Nothing. Just work."

Logan nudged his shoulder. "Come on. Share the wealth."

"Whadda ya want?"

Logan walked back around the desk and took a seat in one of the cushioned chairs. "Bud, you need to get laid if you gotta look at porn on a Monday morning. Must've been a rough *lonely* weekend. Your hand tired?"

Ben gritted his teeth. It had been a rough weekend. After he'd seen Missy at the mall, he'd spent the rest of the weekend flooded with memories of their wild hookup. He wanted her more than he had before they'd hooked up, and now that he'd done the right thing, offering her a job when she needed it most, his stupid libido had ramped up even more. Like knowing he couldn't have her made him want her more. This was what happened when you took the high road —you suffered.

"How's your sweetheart?" Ben asked just to annoy him. That was what Ben called Sabrina ever since Logan claimed she was too sweet for him. She worked in the office downstairs for her relationship counseling practice. Logan had lunch with her sometimes, but insisted, despite their obvious compatibility—the woman laughed at all of Logan's stupid jokes—that they were just friends. Her kind of sweetness—all quiet, doe-eyed compassion—was the exact opposite of what Ben looked for in a woman. Way too much energy required to keep from hurting her tender feelings. That was one of the things he liked about Missy, a tough practical woman, as matter of fact about sex as he was.

Don't think about it! Keep your head in the game.

Logan grabbed Ben's stapler, pulled the top up and fired a staple at him that bounced off his shoulder. "I got us a meeting with Elias Gold."

"No shit? That's great!"

"Yup. January's going to be huge for us. Just watch, all the big-money investors will fall in line once they hear he's interested."

He leaned across the desk and they slapped hands in a hearty handshake. "Fucking awesome. When did this happen?"

"Ran into him in the city this weekend at one of Claire's charity things. Jake talked us up; next thing I know, Elias's assistant emailed me this morning to confirm." Claire was Jake's wife, a movie star moving in elite circles.

"It's early there, isn't it?" Ben asked. Elias was based in California.

"He stays on East Coast time to keep up with the stock market, so his assistant does too."

They grinned at each other.

Ben drummed his fingers on his desk, still smiling. "It's really happening."

Logan set the stapler down and jumped up. "It really is. When's Missy coming in? I've got a huge data-entry job for her. You think she can do some accounting too? I want to start pulling the numbers for our meetings next month and put that all together with some cool graphs of our rise to the top."

Ben shifted uneasily. Logan had agreed by text yesterday to hiring Missy no questions asked because he trusted Ben's judgment. Plus he knew her from a few parties. "I have no idea," he admitted. "You can ask her. She'll be here by one."

Logan stared at him for a long moment. "Are you telling

me you hired an admin and you don't even know what her skills are?"

"She's been an executive assistant for years. I'm sure she has lots of skills."

Logan put his palm out, wiggling his fingers. "Lemme see her résumé."

Ben cleared his throat. "I, uh, didn't ask for a résumé."

Logan's brows shot up. "Our whole company is based on looking into employees' backgrounds and you didn't even get the basics?" He jabbed an accusatory finger at him. "You want her!"

Ben fought to look innocent. He'd never told anyone he'd hooked up with Missy. "She needed a temp job and we needed a temp."

Logan shoved a hand through his hair. "You fucking horn-dog. Keep it in your pants, I mean it. We've got a lot of work to do before January."

Ben clenched his jaw. "I'm keeping it professional. I know we can't afford another mark against me."

Logan gave him a sympathetic look.

"I won't let you down."

"I know." Logan headed out, slapping the doorframe overhead before saying over his shoulder, "Next time I'm doing the hiring."

Missy headed upstairs to Checkin, her new office gig, with no small amount of trepidation. She and Ben had agreed to keep it professional, which was totally the right thing to do, but she knew it wouldn't be easy to deny the attraction. She couldn't say she regretted their hookup, it had been *fantastic,* but it did leave her with a longing for more. Ugh! No, absolutely not. Giving in to the attraction would only lead to something deeper because somewhere along the way she'd moved past lust to real respect and admiration. How many men would be caught dead at a craft bazaar buying a handknit Christmas sweater on behalf of their grandmother? Or spend their

Thanksgiving cheerfully working at a homeless shelter? He'd even helped out a stressed-out elf at the mall, offering her a much more respectable gig. She tried not to think too hard on her short-lived career in elfing.

No, a relationship was out of the question. No man was trustworthy. Hadn't she learned that lesson the hard way, over and over? First with her ex-husband, then with her work at the women's shelter and the crisis hotline, and then with the married Matt. She'd promised herself to deal with men on her own casual terms, a vital part of her plan to stay safe. Part of being a survivor was knowing when to cut ties that could leave lasting damage. After this temp job, she and Ben would go their separate ways on friendly terms.

Their door was unmarked, but the only other upstairs door had a small sign for a Reiki practitioner. She opened the door to a large space with a white round table in the center surrounded by six white swivel chairs. A makeshift kitchen stood in one corner behind a single cubicle wall. Three offices with glass walls faced the central space, with their doors wide open.

She walked farther in, peeking in the first spacious office, where Ben sat behind a modern L-shaped desk with a light natural wood finish and metal legs. He wore his usual long-sleeved Henley and jeans, which fit with the casual tech culture she was used to back in Seattle. She'd worn business casual—navy blue cardigan over a white button-down shirt with dark gray pants—aiming for professional to set the right tone from day one.

He stood abruptly. "Hey, you're here. Let me give you the tour."

"Ah, okay. I think I saw most of it when I wandered in here. Don't you lock the door?"

He crossed to her, close enough for her to breathe in his scent—warm spice, leather, and man. "Why would we lock the door?"

She turned and walked back to the open center of the office, already tempted having him close. "What if you go out to lunch and someone steals all the laptops?"

He stood next to her, brows drawn together. "You're para-noid. It's downtown Eastman. There's just people shopping or eating at the diner across the street."

He headed over to the kitchen corner and she followed, looking her fill at his broad back, remembering the play of muscle under her hands. *Professional, I am a professional.* She shifted her gaze to the back of his neck, still too enticing, and on up to his short-cropped hair that had felt surprisingly soft.

"They have a police department for a reason," she said belatedly.

"So we've got all your basics—" he gestured around him "—coffee maker, microwave, mini fridge. Logan keeps frozen Snickers in there. Eat them at your own risk."

"Because they're old?"

"No, because I don't like to share," Logan said cheerfully, stepping into the small kitchen space with them. Logan was the best looking of the Campbell clan, in her opinion. All of the Campbell brothers were of the tall, athletically inclined variety, but there was a male beauty in his face that was movie-star quality. Warm brown eyes were highlighted by his short light brown hair and sexy beard, his features perfectly symmetric, even his nose was cute. Add in his warm easy-going nature and she was sure he had women throwing themselves at his feet. Not her, though, she liked a man with a bit of an edge, the kind that didn't need sweetness and light in a woman.

The kind she'd have a professional relationship with if it killed her.

Logan offered his hand to her, the height of professional-ism, even in a long-sleeved shirt, jeans, and sneakers. "Good to have you on board. Can you do accounting, graphs, presentation software, data entry, and filing?"

"She just got here," Ben snarled.

"Well, I didn't see her résumé," Logan replied with some bite.

"Yes to all of that," Missy said to Logan.

"Awesome, we can get started right away." Logan gestured to follow him. "Come on."

"I'm giving her the tour," Ben said through his teeth.

Logan grinned and pointed out his version of the tour. "Three offices, kitchen, bathroom, supply closet, done. Missy, I'm not sure if Ben filled you in, but we have some important investor meetings coming up in January, and I'd like to be prepared."

"Of course, I'll get started right away," Missy said.

Ben glared at Logan. "At least let her take off her coat, get situated."

Both men reached for her coat, and she stepped out of reach, taking it off herself. "Just show me to my desk and I'll get started."

Ben turned to Logan and practically growled. "There's paperwork in my office to get her on payroll."

"We'll just cut her a check," Logan countered. "She's only here for three weeks and change. Let's not waste time."

Her head was spinning as the two men faced off over her for some strange reason. "I'm here to work. Let's get to it."

Logan flashed a smile so dazzling she felt herself flush. "A woman after my own heart," he declared. "Priority number one—work." He shot a dark look at Ben. "Later."

Ben grumbled something and then busied himself getting a cup of coffee, so Missy followed Logan out.

Hours later, elbow deep in numbers pulled from reports over the last three years, someone knocked on her open door. She was lucky to have her very own office with a door here and found it much easier to focus on her work. At Marino and Capello Construction and her previous job in Seattle, her desk was out in the open. She hit save. "Come in."

"Coffee break," Ben said, walking in with two take-out cups of coffee.

"You went out for coffee? What's wrong with the coffee here?"

"Nothing. I like to start the week out with the good stuff from Something's Brewing Café." He handed her a cup. "It's their holiday blend. Logan got the peppermint mocha stuff that barely has any coffee in it." He made a face. "Tastes like a chocolate mint with a pound of sugar on top."

"It is super sweet," she agreed. "I love their holiday blend, thanks so much." She wrapped her hands around the warm cup. Her book club met at the café, and she always made sure she was there early enough to get a coffee before they closed. The Happy Endings Book Club was allowed to meet there after hours because they brought in so much business to the attached bookstore, Book It, both owned by husband and wife Shane and Rachel O'Hare.

Ben took a seat in one of the cushioned chairs across from her. Even with a desk between them, she was overheating just having him in her office. Ridiculous. Not only was he out of reach, the door was wide open and the entire front wall of the office was glass, facing the central meeting area. Nothing was going to happen.

"How's it going?" he asked. "Logan working you too hard?"

"Not at all. I like to be busy. Things are dead at my regular job. I'm just doing year-end stuff, wrapping up. This is a lot more interesting work. You didn't tell me you were getting investors."

He sipped some coffee, watching her over the rim. "We haven't talked much."

She concentrated on her delicious coffee, trying not to think of what they'd been doing when they hadn't been talking.

"Did you get a chance to see Sabrina?" he asked.

She smiled. "Yes, we had lunch right before I came up here."

"So what's your deal? You have a roommate or…?"

She tensed. "Why do you want to know?"

He lifted one large shoulder. "Just curious about you."

"I live alone. Planning on stalking me?"

"I don't need to stalk you." He leaned back in his seat. "I keep running into you."

Fate, she thought but didn't say, a little surprised he didn't tease her about it. He was being the professional he'd promised to be. Dammit. She missed warm, teasing Ben. This version of Ben was cordial, but distant. But he did bring her this wonderful coffee on her first day.

She bit back a sigh. "Guess it's no longer fate that we run into each other since I work here."

"Mmm," he said noncommittally. "You don't have to answer if you don't want to…" She tried not to fidget, already dreading whatever he was going to say. "I was just wondering if you'd ever lived with someone, like a boyfriend or husband. I've always lived alone."

Husband? Her gut clenched. She did *not* want to talk about Louis. He was probably holed up in some hovel, all that money he stole already spent on drugs. Just the thought of him filled her with shame. Had Ben found out somehow? He had said he could find out anything on the internet.

"Missy?"

She swallowed hard, heart hammering against her ribcage. "Did you look me up? Digging for dirt on the internet?"

He sipped his coffee. "It was just a question."

"What's with the third degree?" she snapped.

He stood, saying calmly, "No need to get worked up. We're just getting to know each other."

She took in a slow deep breath. "I have a lot of work to do."

He tapped her desk. "That you do. Glad to have you here."

"Thanks."

He left and she stared at his retreating back, wishing she could take back all her defensiveness. She'd driven him away when he'd just been trying to be a friend. She stared at her wonderful coffee. It wasn't a secret that she lived alone. But why had he mentioned a husband? That was always a hot-button topic for her. Was it just conversation, or did he know something? Her sister knew about her marriage, and Missy had mentioned in passing to her friends that she'd been married before, giving no further detail other than marriage was not for her. She supposed it was possible word had gotten out. He probably wanted to know more, just being curious about her like he said. She shouldn't be so paranoid.

She went back to work and didn't stop until six when Ben stood in her doorway again.

"Workday's over," he said.

"Almost," she said, her eyes glued to the computer screen.

"I'm going to have to pay you overtime if you keep going."

She copied and pasted the next column of data, hit save, and left a note to herself where she'd left off. "Okay, done."

He stood on the other side of her desk. "Here." He handed her a check. "An advance so you don't have to worry about helping out that family in time for Christmas."

She glanced at it. Three thousand dollars. They hadn't discussed salary, but this was very generous for three weeks of part-time work, especially in advance.

She handed it back. "I can't accept this. I haven't done the work yet."

"I trust you."

"I don't feel right accepting money for something I haven't done." She pressed it into his hand. "Just pay me when you do the regular payroll. Okay?"

He folded the check in half and tucked it in his back pocket. "Why won't you accept a little help?"

Because I'm the only one I can depend on. "Not necessary." She pulled her purse from the bottom desk drawer and stood.

He gestured for her to go ahead of him through the door. She met his eyes, warmer now when they looked at her, not lusty so much as caring. Like he really saw who she was and liked it.

She moved forward, her stomach fluttering for no good reason, and then something made her stop. Standing right next to him, looking up into those warm blue eyes, she wanted to say…something. She didn't know what. *Thanks again for the coffee and the job, and I really like you? Sorry I drove you away after you were so nice?*

His lips curled into a hint of a dimpled smile. "Yes?"

Her heart hammered because this felt real. Not just lust. So much more than that.

"Night, guys!" Logan called cheerfully.

Missy jumped.

Ben put a hand on her shoulder and gave her a squeeze. "Night, Logan."

Logan stopped outside her office. "Hey, fair warning, the meeting table has a wobbly side, so you guys better stick with the desk."

"We were on our way out," Ben said, giving Logan a good glare. "Go home."

Logan grinned.

Missy felt herself flush. Did Logan know she and Ben had hooked up before? She was not about to ask Ben about it.

The three of them headed out the door, Logan stopping to lock the door behind him.

"Long day, huh?" Logan asked, catching up with her on the steps. "I can already tell you'll be a real help around here."

"Thanks," Missy said. "I appreciate the work."

They reached the bottom of the stairs.

"You want to get a drink to celebrate your first day?" Logan asked her.

"We can all go," Ben said, sounding surly about the whole idea.

Just then Sabrina came out of her office. "Hi, all! How'd the first day go?" Sabrina was back to her girl-next-door look —straight dirty-blond hair pulled back in a barrette at the nape of her neck with very understated makeup around her brown eyes and round cheeks. Missy had been uncomfortable with Sabrina when they first met because Sabrina had just been so sweet and on the quiet side, but as she got to know her, she discovered she had a subtle snarky sense of humor and a loyalty to her friends that Missy really appreciated.

"Hey," Ben and Logan mumbled to Sabrina.

"Great," Missy told Sabrina. "I'll tell you all about it back home." She turned to the men. "Sabrina lives down the hall from me. I'll see you tomorrow."

She walked out the door with Sabrina, leaving the men behind, and headed toward the back parking lot. Sabrina squeezed her arm and said in a low tone, "Major testosterone flare-up. Were they fighting over you?"

"I think they're giving each other a hard time through me. You know the way guys rib each other."

Sabrina shook her head. "Ben's more your type, right? All rough edges."

Except that was just the outside. Missy knew a different side of him, caring and compassionate. Crap. She did *not* want to be falling for him. She didn't want to be falling for anyone.

She forced herself to focus on Sabrina. "I don't know," she said in a teasing voice. "Logan's pretty hot with that beard."

"You think?" Sabrina chirped. "Huh." Like she'd never noticed.

"Yeah, huh."

They cracked up.

"I'll see you at home," Sabrina said, heading for her new car, a sleek white Lexus. Business was good for Sabrina as word spread that she was a true "relationship healer." There'd even been an article in the local paper about her. "Stop by my place. I've got a lasagna ready to pop in the oven." Sabrina was a true domestic goddess.

"Sounds great, thanks."

She slipped into her old Subaru just as Ben and Logan walked out to the parking lot—both of them puffed out, swaggering and badass, neither of them speaking. She imagined they'd just gone another testosterone-fueled round of sparring, probably one of them shoved the other too. Men.

9

———

Tensions were running high at Checkin. For Ben, anyway. Bad enough he couldn't stop thinking about Missy with her sexy-as-fuck mouth talking business with him, her sexy body in those form-fitting button-down shirts and skirts, even her dress pants were making his pants tight. He wanted to bend her over his desk every time she stepped into his office. Wanted to take her home for more wild sex in his bed, in the kitchen, wherever and whenever he wanted it. He felt like a beast straining at professional constraints. Of course, Logan made it worse, getting his jollies razzing Ben in his back-handed way about Missy. Payback would be a bitch.

Missy was the height of professionalism, which only made him feel more depraved. Not that he let any of that show. He stuck to the plan, trying to get to know her. Women loved talking, especially if you asked them questions about them-selves. Not Missy.

Monday: coffee and one Ben question unanswered. Not willing to share she was married before.

Tuesday: coffee and two Ben questions unanswered. Not willing to share her longest relationship. Also not willing to share what she liked to do when she wasn't working.

Wednesday: coffee and one Ben question deflected. Not willing to share where she grew up.

Thursday: coffee and a new strategy. Yeah, he learned. No questions. He'd share and then she'd share. Today he'd crack through those defenses or die trying. To say she was a closed book was an understatement. While he admired her strength, she was so cagey about her past it was starting to worry him, like she was hiding something important. Something he needed to know to understand her. The fact that he couldn't just let it go should've been a red flag. He was getting in much deeper than she was, too invested in connecting with her, for reasons that were frighteningly clear to him—he liked her way too much to be explained away by lust. Halfway to the slippery slope of relationship land given the smallest return of feeling in his direction.

Yup, he had it bad. He was sure it was the chase that had hooked him. For sure if she'd been chasing him, he'd already have moved on. So he had no one to blame but *her* and her cagey ways.

He knocked on her open door, not bothering to wait for a reply, simply moving in with coffee for their afternoon coffee break. Her eyes were glued to the computer screen, biting her plump lower lip in concentration in a move that went straight to his groin.

"Coffee break," he said, setting the take-out coffees on her desk and taking a seat across from her. He always got Logan a coffee too, so it wasn't like he was singling her out. He was just being friendly, which was perfectly fine with a coworker.

She clicked a few more times and looked up, smiling. "Thank you. I could get used to this. Usually I'm the one fetching coffee." She took the coffee and sipped. "I thought you were the numbers guy."

"I am."

"So how come I've only been working on numbers with the tech guy all week?"

He clenched his jaw, not willing to share why Logan was taking the lead on the investor meetings. Missy would never look at Ben the same way again if she knew he'd been accused of sexual harassment, even if he was innocent. Finally, he said simply, "Logan's taking the lead on the investor meetings, so he needs to be familiar with the nitty-gritty."

"I guess I thought it would be both of you. All I've been doing is dropping off copies of everything to you."

He sipped his coffee before saying, "Exciting news for Charlotte and Ty." Their mutual friends were neutral territory. Ty was the honorary brother he'd grown up with, and Charlotte was one of Missy's friends from book club. Charlotte had gone into labor a short while ago. Ty had texted everyone with the news, promising regular updates. Ty was understandably freaked about his first child coming a month early, especially given Charlotte's high-risk pregnancy. She'd been on bed rest the last few months.

Missy beamed. "It is exciting. Charlotte's in good spirits. The doctor says the baby's a good weight and everything should go smoothly. Hopefully by tonight we'll hear the good news."

"That's great." He studied her for a moment, all lit up with talk of the upcoming birth. "Baby's a lot of work," he said casually. He knew this to be true, he'd witnessed first-hand his honorary brother, Alex Campbell, struggle as a single dad with his baby daughter. But he really wanted to know Missy's take on it.

Missy got a soft smile that he'd never seen on her before. It warmed him seeing that crack in her tough shell. "They are a lot of work, but so worth it. I've helped out with my niece, Chloe, since she was born and now Leo. He's six weeks and already smiling." Her eyes got a faraway look. "He smells delicious, all sweet and new."

He didn't know what to say to that. He'd never smelled a baby.

"It's why I moved to Clover Park," Missy said, surprising him by continuing to share openly. "My sister, Lily, wanted me to be part of her family. I adore those kids, probably the closest I'll ever get to being a mom." Her voice had gone soft with longing.

"Is there a reason you can't be a mom?" he asked gently.

Maybe she physically couldn't have them, but they both knew adoption could be a great option.

She straightened and, in an unprecedented flow of words, denied her own longing. "Not that I even want to be a mom. I love being an aunt. Just shower them with attention and get out before you have to change a diaper or deal with crying and all that. You're right, babies are a lot of work." She took a swig of coffee and promptly choked, her eyes watering as she coughed.

"You okay?" In that moment he glimpsed her vulnerability, and everything in him wanted to gather her close.

"Yeah," she choked out. "Must've went down the wrong pipe."

"Most things worth having in life are work," he said.

"Do you want kids?"

"Never really thought about it." He thought about it then, imagining coming home to Missy with that soft smile, a couple of cute redheaded kids excited to see him. "I can see the appeal. And now that I know they start out smelling delicious…" He trailed off with a smile.

She laughed. "Yeah."

"I'd love to meet Chloe and Leo." He wanted to see Missy with the kids she loved so much. He wanted to see that soft look in her eyes, that soft smile.

Her eyes widened. "Oh, that's not necessary."

He set his coffee on the desk. "I know it's not necessary, but they seem important to you."

"They're my family," she said softly.

"And they sound like fun."

She brightened. "They are, but no."

"Come on, we're friends, aren't we? What's the big deal?"

Her expression closed. "The big deal is my sister will get the wrong idea. She'll think you and I are serious when we're not. I've never introduced her to any men I meet."

He looked down his nose at her, playing it up. "You're such a scaredy-cat."

"I am not."

"You act so tough—"

"I am tough," she snapped.

"But you won't even hang out with me," he said smoothly.

They had a staredown and he waited her out.

She swallowed visibly. "You really want to be my friend?"

"I really want to be your friend." *For now.*

"Do you think it's possible?"

"Why not?" he asked, sounding completely casual about the whole thing despite being on edge. Would Missy let him in? This was the only way it could happen. Friends, hanging out, potential for more an excruciating time later.

Her cheeks flushed bright pink and she smoothed her hair back.

Was she remembering their hookup? He kept his mouth shut. That was not workplace appropriate. He wouldn't even make a move outside the office either, not while she was working for him.

She looked at him, her eyes soft. "I—"

Logan barged in. "Hey, guys. Missy, I found those old reports."

Ben left quietly, leaving them to it. He'd put it out there. It was up to Missy to meet him halfway.

The moment Missy had her office to herself again, she slipped out to the bathroom and splashed cold water on her face. Ben was getting under her skin, bringing her favorite coffee every afternoon, being so friendly. She was well aware most guys didn't bother with questions about her, preferring to talk about themselves. If he'd just wanted sex, she figured he wouldn't bother with all the conversation, he'd just make a move. Not at the office, of course, they'd agreed to keep it professional, but surely he wouldn't hesitate to walk her to her car after work and proposition her, or even text her for a late night booty call.

She was so confused. She'd thought she understood men and what they wanted from her. No man had ever wanted to be friends with her. She still wasn't sure if she should take his offer to hang out seriously or if he was playing some kind of game.

She grabbed a paper towel and dabbed her face dry, reason returning to her. She didn't have to figure out Ben's reasons, she just needed to be clear on what she wanted.

She blew out a breath. The problem was, she wasn't so sure anymore.

After work, she was relieved to have plans with Sabrina and Lexi so she could stop thinking about Ben. They were making chocolate cupcakes for after their Happy Endings Book Club meeting in anticipation of the good news about Charlotte and Ty's baby. Charlotte had asked them from the very beginning to stay positive, and this was their way of honoring her request. The plan was: book club meeting at Something's Brewing Café, then over to Garner's Sports Bar & Grill across the street for their usual after-book club drinks, where they'd wait for baby news and celebrate with champagne and cupcakes.

They were a little late to book club because it took time for the cupcakes to cool. Then she and Lexi had formed a chocolate icing assembly line while Sabrina decorated with her pastry bag of vanilla icing, writing in perfect script "baby" and "love," alternating, across the tops.

"No news yet," Hailey, leader of their book club, announced the moment they walked through the door of Something's Brewing Café.

Normally the cozy space with its deep red walls, golden sconces, and dark wood tables filled with the lingering scent of coffee and delicious pastries made Missy relax, but tonight there was a definite tension in the air as they all waited to hear how Charlotte and the baby fared.

"I'm sure we'll hear something soon," Sabrina said in her soothing counselor tone. She set a triple-tiered cupcake holder on top of one of the tables that had been pushed to the edges of the space for their meeting. The women sat in a circle of chairs in the center.

They quickly took their seats. Missy looked around at the

closest friends she'd ever had, all of their faces drawn tight with worry for Charlotte. With Charlotte in the hospital and movie star Claire in California for postproduction on her movie, there were only eight women, including herself.

Mad, a tough blackbelt with a secretly sensitive side, stomped her black boots on the floor as she stood. "What's taking so long? She's been in labor for four hours now."

Carrie, a sweet blonde pediatric nurse, spoke up. "It's perfectly normal, especially for a first child. The baby will come when it's ready."

Mad whipped her head toward Carrie, shoving her dyed red hair out of her eyes. "Easy for you to say. It's not your family." Mad considered Charlotte a sister since she married Mad's big brother Ty.

"Mad," Hailey said quietly.

"What?" Mad snarled, her hands in fists. "She doesn't know what it feels like. I want to beat the shit out of something."

Hailey stood, went over to Mad and spoke to her in low tones before hugging her. They were close in height, around five foot four, their hair clinging together—Hailey's long strawberry blond picking up wisps of Mad's choppy red. Probably static electricity, but Missy couldn't help but think about their close bond. So different—an ultrafeminine beauty queen and tough tomboy—yet so in synch.

Mad pulled away, dashing her eyes with a fist before taking a seat, crossing her arms and slouching low in her seat.

"You know what?" Hailey asked, her pale blue eyes bright. "Instead of talking about *Heart on Ice*, let's talk about Ty's favorite, the Laird trilogy."

They cracked up, even Mad snorted out a laugh. When Charlotte had been put on bed rest a couple of months ago, they had a few of their Happy Endings Book Club meetings in her bedroom, which Ty insisted on attending, saying he was "romance-curious." They all knew he was in full over-protective-husband mode, there to keep an eye on Charlotte and make sure she didn't get overly excited in her delicate state. The hilarious part was Ty really got into the stories and was heavily invested in the discussion of *Highlander's Mission*, and also extremely eager to read the next two books in the trilogy.

"I wouldn't be surprised if Ty started wearing a kilt around the house after that," Missy said with a straight face.

"Yes!" Mad crowed. "I'm totally getting him that for his Christmas present. I picked him for my family's Secret Santa."

"Get pictures." Lexi smiled evilly, a sharp contrast to her usual cuteness, especially with her dark brown hair up in a high ponytail. "Perfect blackmail."

"You're a devious woman," Mad said, reaching over and fist-bumping Lexi.

"It was sad that Brianna had that arranged marriage," Sabrina said, all quiet sincerity. She tucked a stray lock of dirty blond hair behind her ear. "I mean, I know it was common for that time, but it was so clear she was supposed to be with Roan."

"It wasn't all bad," Missy said. "Roan made her his mistress. At least she could be with him, and he did live in the best home since he was the laird."

"It's not like it was an honor," Sabrina returned with a good amount of indignation for the heroine. "Her husband would've blamed her for that. Tensions would've been high in her household."

"Get a grip, girl," Lexi replied, turning to Sabrina at her side. "First of all, her arranged marriage fell apart when the guy died; second of all, it's fiction."

Sabrina cocked her head. "I'm sorry, were we not supposed to take these stories seriously?"

"Of course we are!" Hailey exclaimed.

Sabrina went on, speaking to the group. "Because I always thought there were deeper layers here of love, hope, and redemption. Everything that *matters* in life."

They all got quiet for a moment.

"Oh, shut up," Lexi said, giving Sabrina a playful shove. "We know you're just hot for Roan and his…sword."

Sabrina's cheeks dotted with red. "I'll admit I'm not immune to the appeal of a strong male, who—"

"Is naked under his kilt," Missy supplied.

"And don't forget shirtless," Lexi put in, her brown eyes gleaming. "Remember the cover? He's like—" she gestured to her own narrow shoulders "—massive shoulders, bulging arms, tight abs, and then there's Brianna, all petite and crushed against him. Didn't you just want to be her?"

The women all heartily agreed.

Hailey beamed, flicking her long strawberry blond hair over her shoulder, and began an enthusiastic discussion of Roan, Brianna, and Brianna's badass warrior brothers, who fell hard for their women.

For a short time, they all relaxed, enjoying dishing about one of their favorite reads. Missy had even reread the first book in the trilogy. There was something so compelling about the laird, a formidable foe to his enemies, loyal and compassionate to those under his care—the people in his community and, most especially, Brianna. Oh, shit. She had a thing for that rugged kind of man with deep compassion, didn't she? No wonder Ben was sneaking under her defenses.

When the conversation petered out, all of them subdued again, Hailey called them in for a group hug. "Come on, for Charlotte. We're going to gather all our positive energy and direct it straight to her. Then we'll get a drink in her honor."

"When did you get so woo-woo?" Mad grumbled, but still headed over to Hailey, slinging an arm over her shoulders.

Missy joined the group, one arm around Sabrina, the other around Lexi, her two closest friends, and then was dragged in tight to the circle.

"We love you, Charlotte," Hailey whispered, "and we know you're going to give birth to a beautiful healthy baby boy." They all knew it was going to be a boy.

"And we know you're going to be just fine," Sabrina added.

Missy's throat closed up, the positive words reminding her how much was at stake. She closed her eyes, holding the tears at bay as each woman offered a quiet message of hope around the circle. Missy went last, barely able to speak over the tightness in her throat. "Amen," she said simply.

The women pulled apart, giving each other watery smiles.

"All right, drinks at Garner's," Hailey said, pulling on her long white wool coat. "Mad says the guys are all gathered there waiting to hear news from Ty."

Missy stilled. That meant Ben would be there. Which was absolutely no problem. She just had to pull it together, think positively for Charlotte, and he'd never see her in this vulnerable state. She pulled her coat on. It wasn't like Ben was there to see her specifically. The guys were most likely there because of Josh Campbell, the bartender and manager of the place. He was the oldest of the brothers, along with his twin, but he was local, whereas Jake moved around with his wife, Claire. Josh was subtle about his big-brother role, but Missy had noticed he took care of his younger brothers, biological and honorary, as well as his little sister, Mad. She'd overheard more than once one of the guys speaking to Josh in a confidential tone. And no-filter Mad tried never to piss him off because she said she "owed him way too much." Missy wasn't sure what Josh had done for Mad, but if it was sufficient for Mad to give him that respect, it must've been significant.

A few minutes later, Hailey led the way across the street, talking a cheerful mile a minute about her upcoming Clover Park holiday plans, either trying to keep all their spirits up or mentally preparing for seeing Josh again, which always sent her into a flurry of planning. She was a wedding planner, after all, but with things slowing down for her during the holiday season, she'd planned tons of stuff for Clover Park. This weekend was the first weekend of December, and Hailey had a holiday stroll planned for Saturday complete with ice sculptures, hot chocolate and roasted nuts, strolling carolers, and horse and carriage rides. Sunday was the community tree decorating at Ludbury House, a huge mansion owned by the town, where Hailey worked. Mostly, Ludbury House was host to weddings, but it could be rented out for other purposes. Hailey was not only decorating the large pine tree on the front lawn of Ludbury House, she also had several trees inside waiting to be decorated and then distributed to senior citizens in town who needed a little extra help to enjoy the holidays. And she was wrapping gifts to give to the seniors too.

"Hailey, take a breath," Sabrina advised. "I'll be there to help and so will Lexi and Missy."

"Great!" Hailey chirped. "The more the merrier. How about you ladies?" She rushed forward to ask the rest of their friends. Missy heard Ally agree with great enthusiasm; the others couldn't make it. Ally, a bubbly blonde teacher, was working part-time with Hailey, starting a sologamy business as an add-on to Hailey's wedding planning business. The sologamy thing was pretty cool, basically an empowering ceremony where you marry yourself and vow to honor yourself and seek out your own happiness (as opposed to waiting for some guy to come along like some stupid fairy tale). Missy had loved it when she and her friends had held their own sologamy ceremony a couple of months ago because she knew she could never divorce herself.

Hailey led the way into the crowded bar straight to where Josh stood behind the bar, his dark brown hair more rumpled than usual. "Have you heard from Ty?" Hailey asked immediately.

Missy and Sabrina leaned in close, hoping to hear the answer. Josh made a subtle shake of his head, his lips pressed tightly together.

"Last we heard was an hour ago when Ty went to get ice chips," Clarissa, Josh's girlfriend, said from the bar stool next to Hailey.

Hailey jumped. "Oh, I didn't see you there. That's good to know, thanks." She looked to Josh and back to Clarissa and then Josh. "Can I have a glass of chardonnay, please?"

With unprecedented speed, Josh poured Hailey her requested drink and set it in front of her. Missy couldn't help but notice Clarissa keeping a close eye on him.

Josh turned to the rest of them and said in a subdued tone, "What can I get you, ladies?"

Either Josh was as freaked about Charlotte as the rest of them or he'd changed being with Clarissa. He'd always been laid-back at the bar, but he used to be all charming smiles, quick to tease in a good-natured way, and downright gleeful about locking horns with Hailey. This wasn't the Josh they all knew and loved.

Once they got their drinks, Sabrina asked Josh to hold the cupcakes behind the bar for later and confirmed the champagne was chilling. Satisfied, Sabrina hooked Hailey's arm and guided her to a quiet corner away from the awkward Clarissa and Josh situation. Missy and Lexi followed.

"I'm fine," Hailey said to Sabrina once their little group settled in a small circle, blocking Hailey's view of Josh. "It's all water under the bridge."

"He nearly killed a man for you," Sabrina said quietly, referring to the showdown between Blake and Josh at the *Fierce Loving* wrap party last week.

"He only roughed him up a bit," Hailey said in blithe denial. She took a long swallow of wine. "Don't make a big thing."

Missy and Sabrina exchanged a look. As much as Hailey had spent the last two years looking after their little group, by unspoken agreement, it was time to look after her.

Sabrina was adamant, even raising her voice. "I don't like the dynamics of this situation. It's a classic triangle, and the best course of action is to remove yourself from it. You deserve a healthy loving relationship, not this dysfunction."

Hailey shook her head. "You're making too much of this."

"And I don't like the way she looks at you," Sabrina added. "She's jealous or mad or both."

Hailey flushed pink, took a sip of wine, and then patted Sabrina's arm. "Thanks for having my back, but on to the task at hand. Wait until you see the donation pile back at Ludbury House. You guys, the community has really come together. Tomorrow I've got a freaking truck *full* of food to donate to the food bank, and you should see how many toys we collected for Toys for Tots. The seniors are getting e-readers so they don't have to wait for large-print books to come into the library. They can just increase the font. I even got the librarian over at the Clover Park library to hold a class to teach them how to use them with the e-book library lending program."

"That's awesome," Lexi said.

"That must've cost a lot," Missy put in, thinking of the e-readers.

Hailey smiled brightly. "See what can happen when the community comes together for a great cause?"

Lexi piped up. "We all know it was you who made it happen not the community."

Hailey's lashes fluttered down before modestly claiming, "I might've gotten it started, but they did the rest."

Not only had Hailey reached into her own pocket to buy food and toys (and probably the e-readers too) to start the giving campaign, she'd also taken lots of pictures and posted them on social media and in flyers around town with the headline "Clover Park giving is piling up the joy!" The woman was a dynamo and as beautiful on the inside as the outside, which was a lot.

"You know what, Hailey?" Missy said. "I'm going to volunteer the entire weekend—from setup to cleanup. As long as you're working, I'll be there."

Hailey squealed.

"Many hands make light work," a warm masculine voice said from behind Missy.

The hair on the back of her neck stood up. Ben appeared at her side, flashing a sexy dimpled smile before turning to her friends. "Hello, ladies," he said in a warm honey tone that immediately set Missy on edge. She wasn't about to stand by while he flirted with her friends in front of her. If she and Ben were going to be friends, then there had to be some ground rules—no flirting, no kissing, no *nothing* with another woman in front of her.

Oh, God. I want him all to myself. The uncharacteristic jealousy did not sit well with her.

"Hi," Lexi and Hailey both murmured, looking from him to Missy curiously. She hadn't shared with her friends about their hookup, though they knew she was temporarily working for him.

"Hello," Sabrina caroled.

She worked hard to appear unaffected by Ben standing next to her, but she could feel the heat in her cheeks, her entire body in overdrive, nerves tingling in anticipation. He wasn't even touching her, but the attraction was electric, making her want to throw herself at him. This was terrible.

Hailey turned to Missy, for once not commenting on a possible coupling. "Thank you so much for volunteering. I didn't want to say anything, I mean, it is voluntary, but it's very hard for me to be every place I need to be this weekend. I'd dearly love to have someone working with me the whole time. We'll need to text and call regularly to coordinate all the details."

"Geez, Missy, make us look bad," Lexi said.

"Yeah," Sabrina put in with a smile. "Hailey, you know I'd be there more if I could."

"It's okay," Hailey sang. "It's a busy time of year for everyone."

"Sounds like a big job," Ben said. "I'm in. You need any heavy lifting done, I'm your man." He flexed an impressive bicep. "Or anything else. Missy can vouch for me. I can wash, dry, serve food, you name it."

"Omigod, you're a life saver!" Hailey exclaimed, bouncing up and down on the balls of her feet. "Yes! I'd love to have you there. There's tons of stuff that has to be moved for setup and cleanup. I was going to make do with some wheeled dollies and wagons."

"Wagons?" Ben echoed. "You mean like a kid's wagon?"

"You gotta work with what you have," Hailey said. "I'm very creative that way."

Ben stared at Hailey. "I'll get some of the guys to work the wheeled dollies."

They had an intense discussion of logistics and inventory before settling the scope of the job.

Missy turned to Ben, feeling soft and mushy for this wonderful man who did wonderful things. She'd never met another man like him. She didn't think they existed.

He chuckled. "What?"

"Nothing," she mumbled.

Someone clanged the side of a glass. And then Josh hollered with the voice of a general. "Quiet!"

They all turned to Josh, who had walked out from behind the bar to announce, "Baby's here! Mom and baby TJ are doing great!"

Everyone cheered and hugged each other. Missy impulsively hugged Ben, who hugged her back, lifting her off the ground, making her laugh, her heart soaring with happiness for Charlotte.

Ben set her down and grinned. "I'm an uncle again."

"I'm an aunt again," she said, her eyes watering. She blinked rapidly. "I'm so happy for them."

"Champagne and cupcakes!" Sabrina exclaimed.

Nothing had ever tasted sweeter.

10

Honest to God, Missy took one step onto Clover Park's Main Street on Saturday morning and felt like she'd stepped into a Hallmark Christmas movie. Not that she ever watched them. Much. The holiday stroll hadn't opened to the public yet, so she had an unobstructed view of the charming downtown with its shops and restaurants now aglow in twinkly white Christmas lights. White lights arched over Main Street, wrapped around the trees that lined both sides of the street, and sparkled from every storefront window. The old-fashioned lamp posts were wrapped in greenery with fat red bows. Hailey had even made a huge purchase of wreaths, glittered snowflakes, mini-trees with gold balls, and menorahs, so every storefront window would coordinate.

The street had been closed off to traffic for pedestrians and for the horse and carriage rides. Two carriages, each with one large brown horse wearing jingle bells around their bellies, stood across the street in front of town hall. Already the air smelled sweet and spicy from the hot chocolate stand and roasted nuts cart in front of Something's Brewing Café. She'd checked the roasted nuts out earlier. Chef Shane O'Hare had prepared glazed cinnamon almonds, Mexican spiced chocolate pecans, and sweet 'n spicy mixed nuts. He'd given all the volunteers samples early this morning, and she told him as she had on *many* occasions, after indulging in his glorious coffee, pastries, and homemade ice cream, how lucky they were to have his culinary talent. He'd blushed as red as his hair, mumbling, "Thanks."

But the best part was living this joyous day with Ben.

She wasn't even working directly with him, but every time she caught a glimpse of him in his black down parka, black knit hat, and black work gloves, carrying stuff, she felt giddy. He looked rugged and capable and *hot*.

Now that everything was in place, Ben had joined her to admire their work. He was busy texting someone, so she snuck a look at his strong profile, his angular face with the stubble along his jaw she longed to feel scraping against her. She suppressed a swoony sigh and lifted her face to the sky, breathing in the cold crisp air. The festivities would begin at ten a.m. when the shops opened. It was almost time, and she couldn't wait to see all the kids enjoying themselves. Most families with young kids would be heading to the pancake breakfast with Santa at Clover Park High's cafeteria this morning, a couple of blocks off Main Street, and then head over here.

She turned to Ben, her breath coming out in a cold puff. "The only thing that would make it more perfect is if it snowed."

"We already have the snowman," he said, hitching a thumb down the street. "Ice sculpture."

"Oh, I missed it. Let's go see."

They headed a couple of blocks down to Baldwin Park. The ice sculpture had been set on the grass next to the sidewalk—a huge carved snowman with a top hat and ice carrot nose. Next to the snowman was a snow woman and two small snow kids. Adorable!

Ben checked his phone again. "Hailey needs me to help Marcus and Logan haul a table, chairs, and a couple of barrels from the basement of Ludbury House."

She followed him back downtown. "Barrels?"

"Not sure if she means actual barrels. It's to hold donations to the food bank and Toys for Tots. Tonight we have to help load up the truck and deliver it. Probably be a late night, two different drop-offs an hour away and not close to each other."

That was above and beyond what he'd signed up for and only made her admire him more. "Sounds like a lot of work."

He shrugged. "It's the holidays. Gotta chip in to make it special."

A pang of guilt hit. She'd nearly forgotten about the Harpers between working and thinking so much about Ben. She had to get her priorities straight. As soon as she got her first paycheck, she would start shopping. There was so much she needed to make their holiday everything it should be. She'd already been browsing online, but some things she knew she'd have to check out locally to find the perfect item. Plus she needed to plan a menu, buy the groceries, and buy decorations. Rena had fled their home with only the bare minimum, not wanting to alert her abusive husband that she was planning to leave him with the kids. Missy shouldn't have neglected her work for them this week.

"You're right," she said. "Some work now will make the holidays special later." She'd come up with the menu tonight.

"So after this Hailey doesn't need me until closing time. You want some help at the hot chocolate stand?"

Her pulse quickened, cheeks flushed, stomach fluttering. "That would be great," she said softly.

He stopped walking, a slow sexy smile dawning, his teeth flashing white against his dark stubbled cheeks, his blue eyes warm on hers. "Okay. I'll see you then."

He didn't touch her, yet she felt a radiant glow down to her toes as if he had. Like one of his hugs.

She nodded and lifted a hand in goodbye.

He winked, turned and strode away.

How was she supposed to resist a man as irresistible as Ben?

She couldn't. Not anymore. She wanted more with him—more time, more conversation, and yes, more sex. She'd let him know at the next opportunity.

Ben followed his honorary brother, Marcus Shepard, to the basement of Ludbury House, thinking of Missy. He'd felt something from her back there on the sidewalk, something warm that said she was into him too. Thank God. He did *not* want to be hanging out on a lovesick limb all by himself. Whoa. Back it up. Love? No. That couldn't be possible. They were still getting to know each other. He could count on one hand what he actually knew about Missy, but he was proud to say the look in her eyes seemed more open to him now. If he could just get through the next two weeks and one day without doing or saying anything lustily inappropriate, he'd be all set. Sure, it would be easier if he spent less time with her, rather than all this friendly shit, but he didn't even consider it. He wanted to be with her whether or not things got physical. Damn, this was like a whole new level of enlightenment for him.

He and Marcus quickly located the long wooden table Hailey had requested. She'd taped a paper sign to it that said in black marker: Donation table for holiday stroll. She'd even added a big heart in red marker.

Marcus lifted one side of the table with ease. He was a hulk—tall with a large bulked-up body from his daily workouts—and could probably haul the table by himself. Ben lifted his side, and they maneuvered toward the stairs, Ben taking the lead on the upside, doing more steering than lifting.

He looked down at Marcus's dark eyes with thick lashes staring back at him, his expression not showing the least bit of strain. "You still seeing three women?" Ben asked, curious. The women all knew about each other, and Marcus couldn't seem to pick just one.

"That was a while ago. Keep up with the times."

True. He used to see Marcus regularly for Saturday afternoon basketball games at a park nearby, but they didn't play in the winter, so he hadn't seen him as much. Marcus lived and worked in the city, owner of his own bar in lower Manhattan.

"So what's your deal?" Ben asked. "From three women to zero? Or did you pick one?"

"You sound like Hailey with all your relationship questions." Marcus huffed out a breath. "Could you move faster? The wood is digging into my palm. I think I'm getting a splinter."

That was Marcus for you. He could heave enormous barbells and work his body to the brink of exhaustion, but one little splinter and he was done for. He was sensitive in the oddest ways.

Ben moved faster upstairs as requested. They maneuvered through the doorway and set the table down.

"Right this way, guys!" Hailey called. "We'll be setting up outside Garner's. Josh said it was okay."

Marcus and Ben exchanged a knowing look. Josh, even with a girlfriend, was still wrapped around Hailey's little finger. The part they didn't get was why Hailey didn't know it. Her cluelessness was a real mystery, considering she was a woman hell-bent on bringing couples together, calling herself a "love junkie." It was so obvious Josh was tuned in to her, magically appearing to scare off Blake Grenier at the *Fierce Loving* wrap party, enjoying the hell out of sparring with her at the bar. Once, the guys had all witnessed Josh toss Hailey the basketball during one of their Saturday games when she was *on the other team*. That was when they knew Josh was hooked. Their basketball games had always been fiercely competitive, and no one would purposely give away the ball like that. Why the hell Josh hadn't made his move on Hailey was another mystery. She was beautiful, driven, and smart, though obviously high maintenance, which was why the rest of them hadn't stepped up. More than once, the guys had tried to get an answer out of Josh. The man was a fucking vault.

"Logan," Hailey called, and he appeared right quick from wherever he'd been waiting. Maybe Josh wasn't the only one wrapped around Hailey's finger. "Could you fetch the long four-wheeled dolly out back in the storage shed? I think that would be best for transporting the barrels."

"Yes, ma'am," Logan said and went to do her bidding.

Hailey stared after him and then turned to Ben and Marcus. "He's a sweetheart, isn't he?"

"No," they said in unison. Not because Logan wasn't a great guy. It was just that Logan and Josh were brothers and, if Hailey got between them, it would get ugly.

Hailey flipped her long reddish-blond hair over her shoulder. "Back to work. Would you guys like to wear elf hats?"

Marcus's expression was one of abject horror. "No, thanks," he muttered.

"I'll take one," Ben said, figuring he could put it on Missy and tease her about her previous life as an elf.

Hailey squealed and ran off to get it.

Ben shrugged. "It's for Missy."

Marcus shook his head, a small smirk on his face.

"What?" Ben asked defensively. "We're friends. It's an inside joke."

Marcus smirked even more. "Logan says he wants to retch seeing your lovesick puppy eyes around her."

"I do *not* have lovesick puppy eyes," he said with as much dignity as he could muster. Did he? Shit. Had Missy noticed? That would be embarrassing, especially because he definitely hadn't seen any kind of lovesick look in her eyes.

Marcus gave him a skeptical look. Logan never lied and they both knew it.

"We're friends," Ben said firmly.

"Uh-huh."

"We are."

Marcus spoke in a low tone. "No shame in being into a woman."

Ben crossed his arms, determined that everyone know how professional and just friends their relationship really was. "She works at Checkin. Everything is aboveboard."

Marcus gave him a sympathetic look. "That sucks."

Ben clenched his jaw. It was only for a few more weeks, but he couldn't explain he was waiting for the appropriate moment because what he was really ashamed of was the reason why—the sexual harassment accusation Ashley had leveled at him. He never told any of his friends about that. Unfortunately, some industry people, who could do the most damage, did know. He could not screw this thing up with Missy. Too much depended on him keeping a high profile for the investors. He was playing the long game with a lot more uncertainty in the outcome than he'd like.

Hailey appeared with the elf hat, and Ben took it, grateful to make his escape. He tucked the hat in his coat pocket and then he and Marcus hauled the table across the street and down the block, setting it on the sidewalk in front of Garner's. The stroll was officially open for business, and people had started to arrive, checking out everything. His gaze caught across the street where Missy was serving some kids at the hot chocolate stand.

"Could you get the chairs?" he asked Marcus. "I gotta go." He headed across the street.

"Sure, bail on me!" Marcus hollered behind him.

"Thanks!" Ben lifted a hand and continued across the street. He knew Marcus could easily handle two folding chairs on his own, and Logan would help him with the barrels. He moved quickly, eager to put the elf hat on Missy, but he slowed down as he got close enough to read her expression. She was smiling at the young kids, two boys and a girl, but there was pain in her eyes.

He crossed to her side and took in the kids. Two boys with short brown hair, maybe six and eight, holding their to-go cups of hot chocolate. The girl with long brown hair, about ten, wore a tight pink jacket she'd clearly outgrown.

"It's okay," Missy said to the girl. "Just between us." She smiled. "You like whipped cream?"

"We didn't know it would cost so much," the girl whispered. "Mom only gave us enough for two hot chocolates." She glanced over to where her mom was buying a cone of spiced nuts, but she didn't call to her for more money.

"It's on the house," Missy announced brightly, pouring a cup for her.

The girl's chin snapped up, proud and defiant. "Mom says we work for what we want. I have to earn it."

Missy's smile faltered. "It's for taking such good care of your brothers."

Just then the younger boy hollered, "Hey! You made me spill!" A large puddle of hot chocolate in the street quickly ran into the drainage grate.

"I told you not to open the lid!" his brother hollered. "You made yourself spill!"

"Maddy says there's not enough money for another hot chocolate! Gimme yours!"

"NO!"

The girl hunched her shoulders, her cheeks red. She turned, starting to walk away.

"You with the spilled hot chocolate!" Ben called to the boy. "Did you know hot chocolate is free if you believe in Santa?"

"I do believe in Santa!" the boy hollered, brightening.

"Then you get another hot chocolate." He turned to Maddy. "And you get one too."

"I didn't say I believe in Santa," she whispered.

"You ever make a Christmas list?" he asked, taking one of the carafes of hot chocolate and pouring a cup for the boy jumping with joy on the sidewalk.

"Well, yeah," she said uncertainly.

"Ever sing a Christmas carol?" Ben asked, handing the boy a fresh cup.

"Everyone has," Maddy said.

Missy chimed in. "Looks like everyone gets a free cup." She shot him a grateful look that made his chest puff with pride before turning back to Maddy. "You a whipped cream girl?"

Maddy nodded. Missy piled on the whipped cream, put the lid on, and handed the cup over.

Maddy took the cup, staring at it, her lower lip wobbling. "Thank you." She joined her mom at the nearby roasted nuts cart, her brothers running over to join them, shouting that the hot chocolate was free.

Missy turned to him, one hand on his arm, going up on tiptoe, leaning close, closer than she'd been in a hellishly long week.

He stopped breathing. She was going to kiss him. He could return it if she initiated. His heart thumped hard, the blood surging through his veins. This was okay, really okay, he couldn't be faulted, it was inevitable, they weren't at the office, it was all her and just him returning—

She shifted to whisper in his ear and he nearly groaned. "Those were the Harper kids I'm helping this Christmas. Thank you so much, but I'm afraid word's getting out about the free hot chocolate, and this was part of the fundraiser for the food bank."

He needed to calm the fuck down. If he made it through this professional hell, he should be awarded fucking gentleman professional of the year. If such a thing existed. Now it did. That was him.

He spoke gruffly, pissed at himself for getting all worked up when she was obviously not. "I'll cover it."

"Ben—"

He pulled the elf hat from his coat pocket and put it on her. "I come to the rescue. It's my thing. Now you look elftastic."

Missy didn't react to the hat at all, her gaze drifting over to Maddy, a haunted look in her eyes.

"What's her deal?" Ben asked.

Missy faced front. "There's a line. Let's get back to work."

He had an uneasy feeling over her nonanswer, but there actually was a line. How much were they charging for this stuff anyway? Whatever. It was for a good cause. He could cough up some dough, knowing it brought a little Christmas cheer to Maddy and her brothers. Not to mention contributed to the food bank.

An hour passed and he was starting to get worried about Missy. She barely spoke to him as they worked side by side, becoming more withdrawn, not even smiling at the customers. But then another woman that could only be Missy's sister got in line. The woman was much taller than Missy, but she had the same gorgeous shade of red hair and those lips, the dip at the top with the plump lower lip, were identical. She held a toddler girl on her hip, the girl all bright-eyed, wearing a pink knit cap with a pom-pom over her dark brown hair and a matching pink coat. A tall Italian man stood next to them with a baby tucked inside his black jacket zipped around them both. Just the baby's striped cap over dark hair peeked out. Her sister's husband for sure. The kids had his dark hair.

"Missy!" the red-haired woman called with a cheery wave. "We're here!"

"Hi, guys!" Missy called with a bright beaming smile.

"How's your car holding up?" the guy asked.

Ben turned to Missy. She was having car trouble? He would've made sure it was fixed if he'd known. As a friend. Friends could help each other out.

"Good, Nico, thanks," Missy said. "I appreciate you taking a look at it." She turned to Ben. "My car was making this funny noise whenever I stopped. Nico is a master mechanic. Usually he just works on classic cars, but he made an exception for me."

Nico grinned. "That thing's so old it's already a classic."

Missy laughed. "I know, I know."

Nico looked down at the baby on his chest and started bouncing a bit in place, saying something to the mom.

"That your sister?" Ben asked Missy while they continued pouring hot chocolate, trying to keep the line moving.

Missy's eyes widened. "You can tell?"

"Come on, that red hair? Those lips?"

She blushed, so cute when she blushed. "Yeah, that's Lily. We both took after our biological mom."

He wondered if Missy had been given up for adoption, but her sister kept. Or maybe they both were given up. Now was not the time to ask. Hell, she hated answering questions. One thing he knew about Missy, if he pushed for too much information, she'd pull away. And, really, what more did he need than just to be with her? He already knew the basics from his background check on her. What did the nitty-gritty details of her past really matter?

Missy called to her niece. "Chloe, did you see Santa?"

Chloe nodded vigorously, her pink pom-pom bouncing. "Yes! Pony!"

Nico tapped Chloe on the nose. "Santa doesn't have ponies. Too cold at the North Pole."

"He might have a My Little Pony," Missy offered.

"He might!" Lily exclaimed with great enthusiasm to Chloe. "Remember Princess Celestia and Twilight Sparkle?"

"No. Pony," Chloe said stubbornly.

The parents had a quick whispered conversation.

By the time Lily and her family made it to the front of the line, Chloe was off the pony thing, too busy playing with a small flashlight attached to her dad's keychain. Nico was pacing the sidewalk with the baby. Missy had introduced Ben to everyone. Lily beamed at him and immediately invited him to Sunday dinner.

"Sure, that'd be great," he said, looking to Missy. But her eyes were only for her baby nephew.

"Nico," Missy called, "can I take Leo for a bit? I'm in serious baby withdrawal. You guys can walk around with Chloe, and I'll get him settled in the café."

Nico looked to Lily, who nodded. "I fed him before we left," Lily said. "He's probably ready for a nap."

Nico pulled the baby out of his cozy pouch, still swaddled in a thick blanket, and handed him over to Missy, who immediately started cooing, "How's my little Leo? How's my sweetie-weetie?"

Leo stared at her for a moment before breaking into a big gummy baby smile.

"I'm on break," she called over her shoulder to Ben.

"Yup." Sure, leave him with the line. But he couldn't work up much irritation because she was so obviously thrilled with her baby nephew.

Several minutes later, he caught her eye through the large window of the café, the baby curled up on her chest, seeming to be asleep. Missy looked relaxed and content. She gave him a soft smile that crossed the distance between them and zapped his heart. He couldn't tear his gaze away, heart pounding, something primal in him waking for the first time ever. Missy was a woman meant to have children, and he was meant to give them to her. He knew it like…fate.

And then it started to snow.

He pointed up at it. Missy's jaw dropped and then she beamed.

He watched her staring at the snow coming down with a look of pure wonder. He swallowed over the lump in his throat. A woman who thought snow was magical, who went soft with a baby in her arms.

He'd never seen anything more beautiful.

11

———

Missy spent the next week and a half in frustrated uncertainty. She'd been so sure Ben had definite interest in her at the holiday stroll, but once she'd returned to work at Checkin, he was so distant she'd started to think she'd imagined it. Or, worse, maybe he'd lost interest. She wished she could've followed up on her instincts right after the holiday stroll, but he was busy packing up, and then he was with Logan and Marcus, loading up the truck for their deliveries. Her mind looped with thoughts of Ben. Something in her had shifted, a softening toward him that both scared and exhilarated her. She knew better than to trust a man, but with Ben she wanted to at least give him the benefit of the doubt.

Yes, that was her. Queen of the romantic!

Ben still stopped by for an afternoon coffee break every day, but there was no heat in his eyes. No hint of flirtation in his tone. It was so frustrating because she liked him more than she'd ever liked any man.

Now it was Wednesday morning, her last day was next Monday, and she feared she was running out of time to connect with Ben. They'd both be busy over the holidays, and then who knew how long it would be before she ran into him again? She pushed open the door of Checkin and headed to her office. Logan gave her a quick hello on his way to coffee.

She passed Ben's office and peeked in with a wave. He was on the phone and waved back before resuming his conversation.

That was anticlimactic.

She was being silly. Just because she was feeling differently didn't mean they were about to embark on a whirlwind romance. It wasn't like either of them was looking for long-term. Right? Though lately she'd been thinking maybe they should just see where things went. But what if Ben didn't feel that way at all? Maybe all his friendliness was just the way he spoke to everyone. Hadn't she witnessed him speaking in a warm friendly tone with every man, woman, and child he'd served Thanksgiving dinner at the homeless shelter?

Ugh. This wasn't like her to obsess over a man.

She booted up the laptop and found a detailed email from Logan about her work for the day. He was super organized that way. As always, he was open to questions, but everything was spelled out so clearly she was able to get started right away. She pushed thoughts of Ben from her mind and dove into the presentation software. It felt like only a few minutes had passed when there was a knock at her door.

She glanced at the time, already four o'clock, and looked up, smiling in anticipation of Ben's coffee-break visit.

Logan. Her smile dropped.

He walked in. "Aw, come on, I'm not that bad. Don't look so disappointed."

Busted! Her cheeks burned. "I'm making good progress on the presentation."

"Awesome. I want to put that in report form. Now I'm thinking it'll be cooler to make a video presentation. They'll have the hard copy to do some number crunching, but I want something that reels them in and gives them major FOMO so they'll be eager to sign on the dotted line. You ever put together a video?"

"No."

He crossed his arms, staring off in the distance. "Maybe I should outsource this one." He focused on her again. "Any leads?"

"Try Claire. If not with her production company, I'm sure she knows freelancers looking for work."

"Now why didn't I think of that? My own sister-in-law." He gave her a warm smile. "Have I mentioned you're brilliant? Not just because of that. I've been really impressed with your work."

She looked away, embarrassed. She didn't have a fancy college degree; she'd dropped out of high school and got her GED. Everything she'd learned was self-taught or on the job. Brilliant was not something she'd ever heard applied to her.

"Missy, would you like to join us full-time?" Logan asked. "We could really use someone like you, hardworking, smart, excellent computer skills. It could be a position you grow as the company grows. Maybe we could create an office manager position when we staff up. Just spitballing here. What do you think?"

She shut her gaping mouth with a snap. Holy shit. Two and a half weeks on the job and he wanted her full-time. They were a company on the verge of greatness, and she knew from the numbers she'd been working with that they were already doing fantastic.

"Don't you have an admin returning after the New Year?" she asked.

"Yup, we do. But I'd like to have you here too. She'd do more of the strictly admin stuff, emails, filing, data entry, and you'd do more advanced stuff like reporting, maybe some beta testing as we improve the software, bookkeeping. If you're interested in working on the actual software, we'd pay for coding classes to get you up to speed. Like I said, it could be a position you grow according to your interests. We're not super hung up on job titles. We just want to work with the best people." At her stunned silence, he continued. "Full benefits and stock options. What're you making at your current job?"

She flashed to her bosses, Vince and Sophia Marino, kind hardworking people who'd made it possible for her to move to Clover Park and be close to her sister. Lily had treated her like family from day one, even before they knew each other well, and introduced her to the Marino family and everything good in her life. She owed the Marinos so much. How many times had Sophia told her she didn't know how they'd managed before she arrived? It was about more than money, it was about family. Loyalty. Leaving for greener pastures felt like a betrayal.

Logan tapped on her desk. "Whatever you're making, we'll match it and then some. Think about it." He left.

She sat there for a few moments, her mind reeling. She tried to think logically. This was business, and what Logan had just offered was a great opportunity. The stock options alone could be extraordinary if the company went public. But then emotions took over. She'd have to leave her bosses, who'd become like family to her. Marino and Capello Construction was a good solid business she expected to be around for a long time. They treated her well, even keeping her on at full pay when she worked part-time during the seasonal lulls in their business. If she worked here, her new boss wouldn't just be Logan, it would be Ben as well. Now that would be a twisted and sticky situation—Ben in a position of authority over her. Real authority not just a temp gig, determining her raises and whether or not her employment continued. And, if it didn't work out, she'd have to go crawling back to Marino and Capello Construction, begging for her old job back. She'd lose that warm Marino Sunday dinner feeling of belonging, the only time she'd felt like part of a real family since her parents died. They'd think she didn't appreciate all that they'd done for her.

Nope. Too risky. She'd tell Logan thanks but no thanks.

On the other hand, the job offer was more than she'd ever dreamed for herself, a position tailored to her strengths and interests that could grow into something more.

She turned back to the computer, the screen blurring in front of her suddenly wet eyes. Geez, what was wrong with her lately? She was never this emotional. Gah. Now she couldn't focus. She stood, thinking of going downstairs to spill her guts to Sabrina, who was always a great listener, but thought better of it. Sabrina was probably with a client. She had a regular stream of people seeking her out.

She headed toward the kitchen. She'd get her own coffee today. She was just pouring a steaming mug when the door opened to Ben carrying a tray of take-out coffee for their afternoon ritual. Her heart pounded, and she wasn't sure if it was his sudden appearance—his cheeks ruddy from the cold, tall and gorgeous in his black leather jacket and jeans—or because she'd been caught about to drink coffee behind his back.

"What're you smoking?" he asked her. "Get over here and have the good stuff." He didn't wait for a reply, just kept walking. "Logan, coffee!"

She drained her cup, washed it out, and met up with him in her office. He sat in his usual chair, jacket off, making himself right at home. She fought the sudden urge to sit in his lap, running her fingers through his soft hair—

Nope. He'd been much too distant for her to risk the rejection. Besides, she was a professional. Hadn't she just been offered a fabulous job opportunity on the basis of her professional qualifications? Her stomach rolled and she ignored it. She continued on to her chair and accepted his offered coffee. "Thanks."

He lifted his coffee in acknowledgment before taking a sip.

"Logan offered me a full-time job."

He straightened, eyes wide. "He did?"

"Obviously he didn't check with you first."

"When did this happen?"

"Just a few minutes ago. I guess when you were out getting coffee."

He slowly nodded. "Logan!" he barked. And when he didn't get an immediate response, he grabbed the phone and called him. "You making job offers without my say-so? We're partners." There was a long pause. "True. Yeah, okay." He hung up.

"What did he say?"

Ben cocked his head. "He said and I quote, 'Get your head out of your ass. We agreed she's been a great help and does impressive work. I'll work out the parameters with you later.'" He sipped his coffee, his gaze on her. "I could see it, actually. You in?"

She gripped her coffee cup with both hands. "I don't know. I already have a good job working for good people."

"What're we? The bad guys?"

"No, not at all. You guys have been great." She swallowed hard. "He says my position could grow with the company, beyond admin, whatever I want."

His lips curled up in a small smile. "That's a sweet offer. He knows talent when he sees it and he wants to reward that."

She flushed, uncomfortable with the compliment, her second one today. Brilliant and talented. She told herself not to let it go to her head, but an unusual pride filled her. Recognition of her hard work from her two gorgeous bosses. Uh-oh.

She leaned close to whisper, "You would be my boss."

"And that would be bad because…"

"You know."

His dimples appeared briefly before he got serious. "No, I don't know. Tell me."

Because we hooked up! Because I still want you, and I have no idea if you still want me. "Don't play dumb."

He leaned back in his seat. "You want to work here, you can work here. Absolutely nothing is standing in your way."

Her stomach dropped. He really was over her. He sipped his coffee, quiet and cool, which got her more agitated.

She swallowed hard. "You're just trying to make me say something inappropriate." *I hope.*

He raised a brow, still staring at her, completely composed.

And then she knew how to solve all of her current problems. She'd make her move on Ben now, and whether or not he responded, it would shut down the job opportunity with all its complications. She had a brief moment of hesitation where she considered if there was a better way, but the last week and a half of Ben frustration pushed her forward. She glanced out to the main office area. No sign of Logan.

She leaned across the desk and whispered, "After hours, when Logan is gone for the day, we'll fuck."

He stared at her mouth. "We will?"

She leaned back in her seat, pleased with her elegant solution. Screw professional boundaries, give in to overwhelming lust, and close the door on the job opportunity.

She suppressed a smile, almost giddy at the idea of being with Ben again. Tonight. Maybe right on this desk. Then she thought she should make it sound casual, not put any big expectations out there. She didn't want to scare him away. He'd been very up front with her about the casual nature of his relationships.

She met his eyes. His expression was back to cool and composed. Oh-kay, she could be just as cool and casual. She spoke in a level tone she hoped didn't betray the level of her excitement. "Yes, one more time." *And hopefully more.* "And I will never work for you after this temp gig. You will never be my boss. Ever."

He stood, glaring down at her. "You want to fuck up a great job opportunity for one fuck?"

Cheeks hot, she stammered, "I-I just thought…" She trailed off as he stalked around the desk toward her. Her mouth went dry, all of her senses on alert, excited by his rough edges that she hadn't seen since she started working here, excited that he definitely had some interest in her.

Her chair swiveled suddenly, his hands on the arms of it, caging her in as he got in her face, the heat back in his eyes. "You are *not* fucking me one time."

He was so temptingly close. She licked her lips, staring at his mouth.

He leaned back a little, his voice rough. "I don't care about the job. Do what you want."

Their gazes locked, both of them breathing harder. Heat pooled between her legs, her body on board even before she touched him.

"Then what're you so mad about?" she asked, her voice breathy with lust.

He spoke fiercely, every word enunciated with sharp bite.

"I'm not happy with your casual one fuck."

Her stomach dipped, her pulse quickening. "Say fuck again."

He started to straighten up, away from her, when she grabbed his head and kissed him. He kissed her right back, pulling her up right out of her seat, the fire igniting between them. God, she'd missed this. The rush of excitement, losing herself in his scent and taste. She wrapped her arms around his neck, pressing close against his hard body, primal instinct taking over for a kiss that went on and on. She wanted to merge with him as close as two people could get.

He pulled away abruptly, taking a step back from her. "That was you," he growled. "*You* kissed *me*."

She grabbed the edge of the desk, her knees weak. "I know."

He scrubbed a hand over his face, looking absolutely miserable. Her heart sank, her gut starting a slow churn.

He gave her a hard look. "Dammit, that wasn't supposed to happen."

"Why?"

He spoke through his teeth. "Because I am a professional. I can't move in on female employees. You are a female employee."

"But I—"

He turned and stalked out the door. A few moments later, she heard the door to the main office slam. He'd actually left the office because of her kiss.

She put her fingers to her still-tingling lips, staring at his coffee that he'd been too upset to take with him. A dreadful certainty settled over her. She'd royally fucked things up.

Missy was immediately proven right when Ben avoided her the next couple of days. No more coffee breaks, no more conversation. Just a polite greeting like you'd give any random coworker you passed in the hall. She'd lost him before she ever really had him. She shouldn't have acted so casual, that was what set him off. She'd been hedging her bets in case he didn't feel the same way, and now everything was just...gone. She didn't know if he was more upset that she'd treated him casually or that she'd crossed the line in the workplace. Maybe both. She should've handled it better, waited for a better time to connect with him, somewhere outside of work.

Ben skulked around the office, snapping at Logan, his expression tight. Not at all like the warm teasing Ben she'd enjoyed so much. Logan kept asking him what the hell was his problem. Ben never replied. But she knew it was her. She was miserable over causing him pain when she'd only wanted to bring him closer.

Yesterday, Thursday, she'd told Logan she didn't want to leave her current employer out of loyalty, which he respected. That just made her feel worse. She should've taken that approach all along instead of tangling Ben up in it.

The worst part was, she was running out of time to fix things with Ben. It was nearly five o'clock on Friday, and she had the weekend to figure something out because Monday was her last day, and if she didn't fix it then, she wasn't ever going to get another chance. Maybe after work on Monday she could get Ben alone for a private conversation and try to be more open about her growing feelings for him.

Logan appeared in her doorway. "Got a minute?"

"Of course."

He took a seat and leveled her with a serious look before saying, "Missy, we both really appreciate the work you put in here."

He paused and, in that pause, Missy panicked. Had Ben told Logan she'd acted inappropriately, crossing the line? She'd never done anything like that before and would hate for that to leave a black mark against her. What if he gave her a bad reference? Shit. She hadn't thought through the consequences of her impulsive action. That was so not like her.

She steeled herself for the worst. "Thanks, it's been a great experience."

"Today is your last day."

She gulped. "You're letting me go?"

He slid an envelope across the desk to her. "Full pay. You ever need a recommendation, just ask." He didn't sound mad. Maybe Ben hadn't said anything.

She stared at the envelope and then met his eyes, still not sure what this was about. "So you don't need me on Monday?"

He gave her a small smile. "Consider it an early Christmas gift. Take Monday off, get ready for the holidays, relax, whatever you want." Monday was the day before Christmas Eve.

She nearly collapsed with relief. It was so generous and so unexpected. Still, she had to make sure there wasn't another reason behind the gesture. She knew there was more work to do. "Logan, why? I mean, this is very generous, but have I done something wrong?"

"Not at all." He stood abruptly. "Enjoy your weekend."

"You too," she replied to his retreating back. He'd booked it out of her office.

Hmm…well, it looked like she'd just run out of time to fix things with Ben. It was now or never.

She peeked at her paycheck. He'd paid her in full plus a little extra. Her throat tightened; she'd miss working with Logan. All in all, it had been a fantastic experience working here, knowing her work was appreciated. Except for her screwup with Ben, she had absolutely no regrets. She tucked her paycheck into her purse, stood, and set the strap over her shoulder. She looked around her office, probably the last time she'd have her own private office, and sighed. Then she slowly walked out, grabbing her coat from the back of the door and carrying it, giving herself some time to come up with what she was going to say to Ben.

This wasn't the right place for that kind of conversation. She should ask him to dinner, someplace nice where they could talk and eat, like a date. A real date. A jolt of adrenaline shot through her. She'd never asked a man to dinner and couldn't remember the last time she'd had a real date.

She picked up speed, making the short walk to his office and barging right in before she could lose her nerve.

His head snapped up in surprise. "Hi."

She gripped her purse tightly, her fingers trembling. She took the seat across from him. "Logan let me go. This is my last day, so I wanted to say goodbye."

His brows scrunched together. "I thought you were working through the end of the day Monday."

She lifted one shoulder. "He said it was an early Christmas gift, giving me the day off. He paid me in full."

"And you're okay with that?"

She nodded. "It was a really nice gesture. Now I'll have some time to shop. I might be able to get everything done before the big Christmas Eve rush. This might be the first time I haven't had to shop on Christmas Eve." Her mouth was running away from her, saying everything but the most important thing.

"Did you like working here?" Ben asked, his tone brusquely professional like she was having an exit interview with HR.

"Yes, everything was great." *And I'm sorry I acted like you were just a casual fuck.*

He nodded once. "And you're happy with the way things turned out? No complaints?"

"Nope. I'm happy." *Much happier if I could be with you again.*

"Good."

They looked at each other for a long moment.

She couldn't read his expression at all. She broke the silence, eager to move past the awful distance between them. "So I guess..." *I'm sorry. I really like you.* The words caught in her throat. She wasn't used to being open with anyone, especially a man. She'd spent so much time and energy protecting herself from the dangers of men.

He leaned forward. "What?"

She gripped her hands tightly together. "I was wondering, I mean, if you wanted to..." She stopped and took a deep breath. He surprised her by speaking at the exact same time with the exact same question.

"Would you like to have dinner tonight?"

12

———

Ever since he and Missy kissed in her office, Ben had been swamped with guilt for crossing the line of professionalism, letting the company down, letting Logan down. He was miserable to work with, he knew it, but he couldn't settle down when every time he looked at Missy he was reminded that he'd screwed up. He knew what was at stake here, had reminded himself over and over every time he was tempted. Part of him had wanted to confess to Logan, but he couldn't bear to see the disappointment in his eyes. All he could think about were the worst-case scenarios—what if Missy turned it around and made it sound like Ben was the aggressor? The damage to his reputation would affect Logan's negotiations with the investors. What if she was pissed that he'd been avoiding her, not even bringing her coffee anymore? What if she found out about Ashley and thought he was just that kind of guy, coming after her in the same creepy way? Sure, she'd initiated, but he'd reciprocated and then some. He'd said fuck way too many times. He'd just been pissed that she'd acted like that was all he was to her—a fuck to get out of having to turn down a job offer. He'd been torn up inside, no longer knowing what was the right thing to do, and fucking miserable about it.

And then everything turned around. Logan stepped in

and put an end to his misery, letting Missy go in a gesture of goodwill. He knew in that moment that Logan understood both the cause and solution to Ben's misery. It was a gift for Ben too, and he owed Logan big time. And then Missy had come to him, prepared to ask him out. He could hardly believe it. From absolute misery to elation in five minutes flat. That was the effect Missy had on him.

He showed up at her apartment door that night and rang the bell, a bouquet of red roses in hand. He was doing it up right, showing her how much she meant to him.

She opened the door, her eyes immediately darting to the roses he held up to her, her expression clearly astonished. She looked at him, her brows scrunched together in a clear WTF reaction.

He nearly laughed. "For my beautiful date."

She stared at the flowers again. Had she never received flowers? She must've been seeing some real losers before.

He reached out, lifting her hand and placing the bouquet in it.

"Ben," she croaked, her eyes shiny, "thank you."

"Are you crying?" he asked, shocked that flowers could make tough Missy cry.

"No!" She hid her face in the flowers and backed away from the door.

He followed her in and pulled her into his arms. She rested her cheek against his chest, wetting the soft cotton of his shirt. He tightened his hold, feeling protective of her surprisingly soft side.

She sniffled and finally lifted her head, trying to rub his shirt dry. "Sorry about that."

He smiled and said in a teasing voice, "Here I've been thinking you're so tough, and then you fall apart over some flowers."

She smiled back, her eyes still watery. "Shut up."

He tipped her chin up and kissed her gently, thrilled to be able to touch her again guilt-free after denying himself so long. "Come on, I'll take you to a nice dinner."

Her lips pressed tightly together. "I'm really sorry I crossed the line at work."

"It's fine. I was more mad at myself." He rubbed the back of his neck. "It was just really important to me I keep things professional in the workplace." He'd tell her why later, but not now. He just wanted to enjoy their first date.

She nodded, fingering the petal of a rose. "And I'm sorry I acted so casual about fucking you one time. I'd like more than that."

Heat surged through his veins. "Dinner first; then you can decide if you want to spread your legs for me later."

She looked up at him, her eyes direct. "It's a done deal. I don't need a nice dinner."

"You definitely do. Don't make me bring you jewelry. A real sobfest around here." He smiled down at her, stroking her cheek with his thumb. "What am I going to do with you?"

Her eyes went soft. "I don't know."

He kissed her and then entwined his fingers with hers. "Let's find out."

Missy started the night flustered, clutching her bouquet of red roses with white baby's breath, breathing in their heavenly scent before going to the kitchen and putting them in the vase from the birthday flowers her sister had sent. No man had ever given her flowers. Even Louis, her ex-husband, hadn't, saying they were a waste of money because they died.

She pushed thoughts of Louis out of her mind. This was her first real date in a very long time and she wanted to enjoy it. She wore her favorite white cashmere sweater, a gift from her sister, with a black skirt, black tights, and black strappy heels. She was glad she'd dressed up because Ben had too, wearing a dark blue button-down shirt with gray pants and dress shoes. It felt like the beginning of something real, and that filled her with more excitement than fear. She couldn't completely banish her fear of relationships, but this date was a huge step forward for her, all because of Ben.

She stepped out of the kitchen and took her coat from the front closet, sliding it on. "All set."

He took her hand, lifting it to graze his warm lips across her knuckles, sending a tingle through her. She felt herself flush, not used to so much sweet affection. "Aren't you cute being all shy," he said in a silky voice, his blue eyes dancing with amusement.

She stared pointedly at her hand still captured in his. "Aren't you cute being all Romeo."

He barked out a laugh, entwining his fingers with hers. "I thought about bringing you candy—"

"Don't." Louis's peace offerings had always been candy. False sweetness to lure her in again, trusting a man who didn't deserve her trust.

"You don't like candy?"

"No."

"Good thing I didn't bring it. I thought it might spoil your appetite. There's this great Indian place. You like spicy food?"

"I love it."

A small smile brought out the dimples in his stubbled cheeks. Gah, those dimples would be the end of her. "Awesome. See, I'd know this kind of thing if you actually talked to me."

She headed downstairs with him, enjoying holding hands. "I talk to you."

"Tiny bits. Glimpses into Missy. I want the whole enchilada."

"How about the whole samosa?" The spicy pastry was much smaller than an enchilada.

He grinned. "That's a nice appetizer. I'll take it."

Warmth radiated through her body just being close to him, the world taking on softer hues, the streetlights glowing, the moon luminescent. *She* was glowing. He made her feel good, safe and loved. Maybe he didn't intend to make her feel loved, but somehow he reached into her heart, wrapping it with warm comforting care. Probably all in her imagination, but it felt like mushy love, and she'd had precious little in her life. She decided not to fight it, for once just to enjoy what he offered.

When they reached his black BMW, he opened the passenger-side door for her and shut it behind her. Wow. He'd pulled out the gentleman treatment tonight. Nice!

He slid into the driver's seat. "C'mere." He didn't wait for her to move, just hooked his hand around the back of her neck and brought her in for a scorching kiss. It was raw and carnal and she never wanted it to end, drowning in a rush of desire. When he finally let her up for air, he murmured, "Just getting the awkward goodnight kiss out of the way."

Breathless, she finally managed to say, "That was awkward. Thanks."

He grinned, put the car in gear, and backed out of the space. "There's the fiery redhead I know."

"Ugh with the red hair. Why're you so into that?"

He drove at a sedate pace through the parking lot, heading to the main road. "It speaks to me. Maybe in a former life I was a Scot hooking up with a redhead. Supposedly my birth mom was part Scottish."

A shiver ran down her spine, the mystical feeling of fate once again unnerving her. "So was mine."

"What was your birth mom's name?"

"Taylor Carson."

"Mine was Margaret Beatty." He grinned. "At least you're not my sister."

"At least we have that."

He reached over and squeezed her thigh, his hand warming her through her thin tights. "Maybe we've got karma *and* fate going for us." His fingers slid a fraction closer to her inner thigh, and she spread her legs instinctively, needing more.

"Maybe it's all hormones."

He slid his hand away, and she let out a frustrated breath.

He chuckled. "There you go making me feel dirty again. Damn, woman, I can't wait to bury myself deep inside you again."

She sucked in air, surprised at the dirty talk when he was

going all romantic on her. He was unpredictable, sexy, edgy, and sweet—a lethal combination to her defenses. Absolutely irresistible.

She spoke bluntly, hoping to throw him off whatever game he was playing with this romantic stuff. If this was just about sex, then she needed to mentally prepare, shields up. "Why not just skip dinner and get right to the fucking?"

A small smile played over his lips. "Now, Missy, what would be the fun in that? Anyone can fuck. We're taking it to the next level."

Her heart caught in her throat. "And what level is that?"

"Mutual attraction, respect, and admiration."

Her stomach fluttered, heart pounding, skin hot. It wasn't just sex, he respected her, admired her even. And it truly was mutual.

He glanced over at her. "Nothing to say to that?"

"Tha-that's nice," she stammered, her neck and cheeks burning. She powered down the window and tilted her head into the cold breeze, mortified to be reduced to stammering and blushing.

"You must be part Irish setter," he said. "You know, red fur, sticking your head out the window."

A-a-and she was back. "Gee, thanks."

"Hey, I'm a horny dog, so it'll all work out." He hit the button to close her window. She pressed hers at the same time and the window halted.

"It's freezing," he said, still pressing his button. "Come on, let go."

She kept her finger on the button, the window still halfway open. "Maybe I wasn't done with the fresh air."

"Have it your way," he said. "Next time I'll bring a parka."

Her heart squeezed. *Next time.*

Once at the restaurant, Spice Jewel, a beautiful place decorated in gold and red tones with dark wood tables and a warm cherry hardwood floor in the wealthy town of Greenport, Ben was back to being her romantic date. And she let him. He helped her off with her coat, pulled out her chair for her, and advised her on the best thing to try on the menu. He probably went here regularly with dates, but she didn't care who he'd been with before because right now all of his warm affection was directed at her.

"We have to get the samosas," he said, smiling at her from across the table. "You did promise glimpses into Missy for every samosa I eat."

She laughed. "I don't remember it quite the same way."

"You said not the whole enchilada, just a samosa. So…"

"There's not that much to know. Really."

"Says the mysterious one."

She shook her head and lifted the menu. "You want to order a few things to share?"

"Absolutely."

They settled on his recommended chicken goan curry, which was a spicy coconut tamarind curry, and saag, which was lamb with spinach and ginger. That would've been plenty for her, especially with the samosas, rice, and naan, but then when the waiter arrived, Ben threw in butter chicken and kaali daal too.

"Ben, that's way too much food," she said once the waiter left.

"I can easily polish it off."

"How in the world do you not put on weight when you eat like that?"

He leaned in conspiratorially. "Truth?"

She leaned in. "Yes."

"Most of my calories are consumed when I eat out."

She leaned back. "You don't know how to cook?"

"I do. I choose not to."

"Why? It's less expensive and healthier."

His lips pressed into a flat line, serious now. "It became a chore for me. Growing up, my mom had a lot of terrible migraines from the brain cancer, so I was the one that cooked and sort of ran the household. Now that I don't have to, I want a break."

Her throat tightened with raw emotion. "I'm sorry. I totally get that. Sometimes you need to start fresh."

He nodded once. "You ever start fresh?"

Many, many times. Starting over at her aunt's house, on the streets, in several foster homes, in her married hell, out of her married hell, in Clover Park. She swallowed hard, telling herself to try to be more open. "Yes."

He studied her, long moments ticking by in silence. "That's it? Just yes?"

"Yes."

"Hmm…"

She smoothed her napkin in her lap, folding the corner of it up and back, up and back.

"So what's the deal with Sabrina?" he asked.

She straightened, relaxing again, glad he hadn't pushed her for more. "What do you mean? Sabrina's great."

"She single?"

She narrowed her eyes. "You seriously taking me on a date and planning your next date with one of my closest friends?"

He crooked his finger at her. When she didn't move, he said, "C'mere, I have a secret to tell you."

She rolled her eyes and leaned in. "What?"

He held her by the chin. "I want you and only you for as long as you'll have me."

Her lips parted in surprise.

His fingers released her chin, stroking lightly down her throat. "Got it?"

She nodded, eyes stinging, and leaned back.

One corner of his mouth lifted as he gazed into her eyes. "You're such a softie."

She frowned. "I'm just not used to, you know, sweet stuff."

"Sweet stuff? Are you calling me sweet stuff?" He pulled out his wallet and removed a business card, holding it up. "Can somebody take my man card?"

She laughed. "Put that away!"

He grinned and tucked it back in his wallet.

"To answer your question, yes, Sabrina's single. You thinking of Logan? They do have lunch together sometimes. He's single, right?"

"Yeah." He shoved his wallet back in his pocket and gave her a wry look. "Have you heard her laugh at his stupid jokes? What woman laughs at a *Monsters, Inc.* impression—" he made his voice high and scratchy "—'I'm watching you, Wazowski, always watching.' Seriously, no woman in her right mind would think that was funny unless she was into him."

She cocked her head. "Well, if it's a good impression—"

"It's a kids' movie!"

She thought about her friend. "Sabrina's kind of an expert on relationships. She's helped so many people find their way to satisfying relationships in her counseling practice. If she hasn't given him the signal, it's because she doesn't think he's a good match for her relationship-wise."

"Wazowski," he returned, as if that said everything.

"Hmm…well, he is really hot with that beard." She lifted a hand at his scowl. "And I say that objectively. It's simply a fact most women would agree on. I'll refrain from listing the rest of his hot features, but, trust me, he's got 'em. Maybe she finds that intimidating."

Ben pursed his lips. "That fucking beard. I told him to shave it. Hipster wannabe."

"He doesn't have sexy dimples to show off like you."

He rubbed his stubbled jaw. "You like that?"

She smiled. "Yeah, I do."

"My grandmother says they make me look like a cutie patootie."

She burst out laughing.

"Of course, that's just when she wants to butter me up," he added, which made her laugh more. "Alright, that's enough. Geez, pull yourself together."

Luckily, the samosas arrived and she was able to calm down again.

Ben lifted one. "Now tell me something about Missy, or the samosa gets it."

"The samosa gets it."

He took a bite. "No sympathy for the plight of this fried bit of heaven, eh?"

She took a bite and chewed. "I'm not sure what you want to know."

"Anything. It's like pulling teeth with you."

"Okay, okay, my favorite color is green, I don't like sweets except cherry vanilla ice cream, I love snow, and my absolute favorite movie is *The Terminator*."

His brows scrunched together. "You like guy movies?"

"There's no such thing as a guy movie or a girl movie. It's just a movie and I like it."

"That's not really your favorite. You're just saying that because you're with me. You probably tell your friends you like a chick flick."

"It really is!"

"Why?" he asked, his voice full of challenge.

"Because she's a total badass doing everything she can to save her son," she fired back.

He gazed at her with deep affection before finally saying, "Thank you."

She looked away, embarrassed for some reason. "No big," she muttered, taking another bite of samosa.

Ben must've sensed her discomfort because he didn't press for any more information, instead making her laugh with stories of growing up with the Campbells and the other guys who'd been taken under Mr. Campbell's wing for one reason or another. Her favorite story was when a hulking teen-aged Marcus took in a tiny white kitten he called Bitty Kitty, hiding it in his jacket pocket, trying hard to cover up the occasional meow by fake sneezing. She could just imagine Marcus with a kitten in his big paw. The best part of the story, though, was Ben helping Marcus out by bringing the kitten to Ben's grandmother, promising Marcus full visitation rights. Marcus couldn't keep the kitten at his apartment since they weren't allowed to have pets. Apparently, Marcus had visited Ben's grandmother for years, bonding over their shared love for Bitty. It spoke to Ben's deeply compassionate nature, even as a teenager, that he stepped in to help Marcus find a way to keep his kitten.

After dinner, Ben drove her home, both of them quiet. The radio was on, soft Christmas carols playing in the background. Full and content, she never wanted the night to end. He'd shared quite a bit of his life growing up, and it made her feel close to him.

"I grew up in California," she blurted in an attempt to share like he had.

He glanced at her. "Okay," he said slowly.

"That's why I love snow. It's still new for me, and it feels like a miracle every time. Soft magic falling from the sky, making everything shiny and new."

"Never thought about it quite like that. It was great as a kid, especially getting the day off school. Now it's just there, something to shovel and clear."

"You're lucky you grew up with it. You probably got to go sledding, make a snowman, have snowball fights."

"Snowball fights are the best. Next snowstorm, we'll have a snowball fight."

She found herself smiling. "Awesome." She liked the way he talked about "next time" with her. Like he wanted to stick around for a while. "When we get to my place, why don't you come up?"

"Way ahead of you, Missy. I come prepared. Condom in my pocket."

She laughed. "Just one?"

"Three, actually. I've been fantasizing about you for an excruciatingly long time. Basically since the last time."

Her stomach did a topsy-turvy flip. "Oh."

"Yeah, oh. First time might be fast and furious, but then I want to slow things down. If you could just keep from going animal on me—"

"Animal!" she cried.

"You're like wrestling a sexy alligator, all claws and snapping teeth, rolling around with me."

She burst out laughing. "You really need to work on your compliments. First I'm an Irish setter, then I'm an alligator?"

"I call 'em like I see 'em."

"I just like what I like."

"I like what you like too. But I think we can manage a slow fuck, sort of build to a monster orgasm."

"Yes," she breathed. "That sounds good."

"I so want to finger bang you right now, but it's dark and I should focus on driving."

She whimpered, drenched with desire.

"Like the dirty talk, huh? I got plenty."

"Hold that thought. You're driving me crazy and I've got to wait for at least a twenty-minute drive."

That only encouraged him. He kept up the dirty talk, telling her everything he wanted to do to her, every fantasy he'd had about her, making her ache with need.

This had to happen fast.

13

Missy had barely gotten her apartment door open when they slammed together, mouths fused, hands grabbing, rushing inside her apartment. He hiked up her skirt and stripped her tights and panties off. She lost her balance because she was trying to get his pants off. He caught her in his arms, lowering her the rest of the way to the floor, kissing her ravenously. They were animals and she didn't care. She worked her hands between them to undo his button and zipper, and he lifted his hips to give her access.

He tore his mouth away, grabbed the condom and got it on in record time before returning to her, sliding between her legs and thrusting inside.

She threw her head back in bliss, the joining one she'd craved for too long. She hung on as he pumped hard and deep, closing her eyes, letting go of everything but the feel of his hot skin, the deep pressure as he filled her; his scent, spice and sex—all of it consumed her. His hand slipped under her ass, lifting her for a deeper penetration that rocked her, the sensations overwhelming, building and building and building, and then she cried out, the explosion of pleasure from her center radiating out. He followed only a moment later, clutching her tight against him.

A long moment later, he lifted his head. "That was the fast and furious."

She couldn't help her goofy smile. "We're animals."

He nipped her bottom lip. "Next time we'll make it to the bed."

"How long for that?"

He grinned. "You want to know how long until I can get it up again?" He moved a slow circle inside her. "With you, not long at all."

She beamed.

An hour later, after an excruciating long bout of foreplay —all Ben's doing, the man was the worst tease—they finally got down to serious business. In her bed. Her on top.

He cupped her ass and gave her a sexy smile. "I know you like being on top, but if you're doing your animal thing, this won't be a slow fuck."

"I'll go slow." Which she did at first, but then it felt so good she couldn't help but speed up, letting herself get noisy, enjoying the hell out of the ride.

He grabbed her by the hips, stilling her. "Changing positions. Keep your knees where I can see them."

She would've laughed if she wasn't so close to the release she craved with every cell in her being.

He flipped her under him, thrusting in slow and deep, his hand coming up to cradle her cheek. "You're so beautiful. These sexy lips." He kissed her lips. "These sweet blushing cheeks." He kissed each of her cheeks. "This cute nose." Another light kiss.

"Fuck me." She arched her hips up.

"This jaw." He kissed her jaw, shifting to nuzzle her neck, bringing hot shivers. His voice was gravelly. "Slow this time. Give me that, okay?"

Hot tears stung her eyes for reasons she couldn't comprehend. She squeezed them tight together.

He kissed her closed eyelids softly. She opened her eyes and he wiped a tear from her cheek with his thumb.

She turned her head away, embarrassed.

He cupped her jaw and turned her back to him. "I like this

side of you, all soft and tender. You don't have to hide from me."

She glared at him, and he merely chuckled, saying, "All right, then," before resuming slow thrusts. Their gazes locked and she didn't turn from the tenderness she saw there, and maybe she had a little tenderness too, because everything felt different. Magical. Beautiful. Glowing. This wasn't fucking. He'd been trying to make love to her, and for the first time in her life, she knew what that meant.

She grabbed his head and kissed him, pouring all she felt for him, all the mushy tenderness and passion, into that kiss. He returned it with equal passion, lighting her up inside. Finally, she broke the kiss, breathless.

"Yes," he murmured, pumping faster, his breath mingling with hers. Her heart drummed in her chest, the pleasure he brought escalating, bringing her closer to him, merging together body and soul. And then a starburst of pleasure radiated through her, leaving her trembling and breathless. His teeth sank into her neck, jolting her and exciting her at the same time, as he pumped into her hard and fast. She went over again in another rush of pleasure along with his release.

He gave her some of his weight and she hugged him. She'd never hugged anyone after sex. It just felt right.

After a moment, he lifted his head and brushed her hair back from her face. His eyes were questioning—their connection so deep she understood. And, for the first time with a man, thought maybe he understood her too. He wanted to know if she was okay, wanted to know if they could have more, wanted to know if he could stay.

She nodded.

He kissed her tenderly. "Thank you."

She was falling for him. It scared her, but she felt too good to fight it. For as long as they had, she just wanted to enjoy him. She reached over and turned off the light on the nightstand.

He settled the covers over them and wrapped an arm around her shoulders, tucking her into his side. She settled her head on his chest, listening to the solid thump of his heart.

He dropped a kiss on top of her head. "I've never had a serious relationship. Thought I should just put that out there."

She turned the light back on to look at him, shocked he'd actually said the words "serious relationship." Most men could barely think relationship let alone say it out loud. His expression was relaxed, his eyes holding hers with a steady gaze.

"Is that a warning?" she asked.

His lips curved. "I'm just saying I'm probably gonna fuck up at some point."

"So you'll refer back to this conversation? Kind of a free pass?"

He laughed. "I told you I'm new at this. See how I already pissed you off?"

She kissed him soundly on the mouth. "I'm not pissed off at all. I'm…happy. I've—" she swallowed hard "—I've never felt this way before."

He gave her a small squeeze, his eyes warm on hers. "Me too."

She turned off the light and snuggled back against him.

Ben spoke in a gentle tone. "Can you tell me why you got upset when I held your wrists the last time we had sex?"

Her glow receded, cold stealing through her. She said nothing. The fact that she'd been with a man like Louis, staying with him way too long, been a victim, it filled her with shame. She knew it wasn't her fault. She'd fought hard to rise above it. But there it was—humiliating shame. A reminder of the high cost of love. One that made her want to pull away from Ben and flee.

"Missy, I sense something bad happened to you, and I just want to avoid any triggers that might send you back to reliving the experience. It's only because I care about you."

Adrenaline surged through her, her breathing rough, her skin clammy. His words were close to what a social worker might say or a counselor. He must've understood traumatic situations more than most people because of his social worker mom. She reached down deep, fighting every defensive instinct, searching for the words that wouldn't reveal too much. "I don't like my wrists restrained," she whispered. "And no hair pulling." Or slapping or yelling.

His arms tightened around her. "What happened?"

Her throat clogged, making it impossible to share more.

"You can tell me anything. No judgment."

She tried to roll away from him, but he pulled her back in tight. She didn't fight him. Some part of her needed him close right now.

"Okay," he said in a soothing voice. "It's okay. I know enough."

She tried to relax again, but it was impossible. Part of her wanted to run far away and hide. How could she crave this intimacy yet fear it? She didn't know how to open her heart and still feel safe.

"Missy, you sexy alligator, I need a hug after you wrung that monster orgasm out of me. Climb up here."

She laughed a little as he pulled her fully on top of him and wrapped her in one of his radiant loving hugs. Long after she would've pulled away, he held on, until finally she relaxed again and drifted off to sleep.

Ben couldn't get enough of Missy. He spent the whole weekend at her place. They even cooked dinner together Saturday night, and he actually liked it. Everything was great. Beyond great, everything was perfect. That worried him because nothing was ever that perfect. But did that stop him? Hell no. Some force greater than himself pushed past all his defenses and kept him close to her, closer than he'd ever been with a woman. And he knew the feeling was mutual because she welcomed him with open arms and soft smiles.

Now it was late Sunday morning and they were cuddled together on her sofa, watching a Hallmark Christmas movie, his man card hiding somewhere at his place. He couldn't care less about the couple on the screen decorating a Christmas tree. All he cared about was the woman in his arms, tough and strong, yet moved by sappy movies and babies and sweet words. He wanted to bring her home to meet his grandmother. Maybe on Christmas Eve; it was only two days away.

He dropped a kiss on her head, waiting for the commercial to ask her about Christmas Eve because he was that awesome of a boyfriend. Finally, the commercial came on, and he tipped her chin up toward him. "What're you doing Christmas Eve?"

"A lot. I've got to wrap the Harpers' presents, prepare the food, pick up a gift card, and then I have to get everything over to them and set up. It's a surprise, did I tell you that?"

"No."

"Well, it is."

"You're doing a lot for that family. What's their deal?"

"It's not just me," she said, dodging the question and not for the first time. "It's from everyone at church. Everyone contributed toward raising the money."

"And then you earned even more. You sure you don't want to work for us?"

She gave him a soft smile. "I love you guys, but I also love my family. The Marinos mean everything to me. They brought me on because they have a long history of family-run business."

He swallowed hard. Did she just say she loved *him*, or was that just a casual I-love-everyone thing?

She kissed him, a quick peck, and turned back to the TV. He stared straight ahead. Should he tell her he loved her? He was pretty sure that was what had taken over his brain. Why else would he have endured three weeks of blue balls just getting to know her as friends? Why else would he actually enjoy cooking dinner with her when it was normally a dreaded chore? Or enjoy cuddling on the sofa, watching chick flicks? But maybe it was too soon for love. Four weeks and change of intense attraction, maybe more if you counted running into each other and flirting regularly before that.

Maybe this was just advanced lust. They did have a lot of

awesome sex this weekend, and he'd spent the night, twice, with zero problem sleeping. He'd only ever spent the night with his ex to avoid a big fight. He supposed he could stop having sex with Missy and see if he still felt good about cuddling and watching chick flicks. That would be a sure sign of love.

Nah.

No good could come from depriving himself. Like he could keep his hands off her. As it was, his hand spanned her flat stomach under her sweater and would be slipping up to the front hook on her bra or down her pants any moment. He hadn't decided yet. Down the pants would be a fast fuck, which was always awesome, but up to her breasts could be a slow seduction that made her come undone. Decisions, decisions.

Someone pounded on the front door and she jumped.

"You expecting someone?" he asked.

"No," she whispered.

He untangled himself from her body and stood. "I'll go see who it is."

She turned off the TV, her arms crossed.

"Missy!" a man's voice barked. "Answer the door!"

Ben frowned, turning to Missy. The color drained from her face. "Who is it?" he whispered.

She shook her head, shrinking into the corner of the sofa.

The man pounded so hard the door shook.

"Who is it?" Ben barked at the man.

"Who're you?" the man asked belligerently.

"What do you want?" Ben hollered.

The doorknob jiggled. The chain was on, but if the guy was big enough and determined enough, he might be able to bust through.

Ben turned to Missy. "Call nine-one-one."

"No," she said in a small voice.

He stared at her for a moment. She was visibly shaking, cowering in the corner of the sofa. This was not the Missy he knew. What had this man done to her?

"Go away!" Ben hollered through the door. "We called the

cops." He felt his pockets for his phone. Must've fallen out on the sofa. He rushed to the sofa, and Missy leapt out of it like he was about to attack her. "Easy," he said, holding up his phone.

The idiot outside kept alternating pounding on the door, jiggling the knob, and then throwing his weight against the door. "You owe me!" the man hollered.

Ben had only hit one digit on his phone when Missy ran to the door and yanked it open, the chain preventing it from opening all the way. Ben rushed to her side.

"I owe you nothing!" Missy yelled so loud her voice cracked. "You stole their money, you bastard."

The man's tone immediately changed to sweet and coaxing. "Missy, honey, I just need a little to tide me over. You do owe me for putting a roof over your head. Three years of rent ought to cover it." Ben would bet everything he had that this was Louis, her ex-husband. Three years of rent, three years of marriage, it fit.

Missy slid the chain open so fast, Ben didn't have time to react. The door opened to a tall, thin man with long greasy black hair hanging in his haggard face. He wore an army jacket and dirty black pants. He looked strung out, needing his next hit, and smelled like he hadn't showered in a month.

The bastard held out his palm to Missy. "I'll settle for a grand. Hurry up and I'll get out of here."

Ben moved forward. "Leave now."

Unbelievably, Missy shushed Ben and then turned to Louis. "I don't have any money. Leave."

"Liar!" Louis yelled, rushing at Missy.

Ben reached for the guy's shoulder to haul him back, but Missy was faster, moving toward Louis, grabbing his shoulders and sending her knee up into the man's groin with such force he dropped like a stone, curling on the floor and moaning.

Ben was ready to drag Louis out the door, but Missy stopped him with a hand on his arm. Her eyes were red fury.

She jerked Louis to his back, dropped a knee into his chest that made him groan, and then slapped him. Hard. "You ever come near me again," she shouted in his face, "I will castrate you! Do you understand?"

Louis said nothing, looking like he was about to lose consciousness, probably from pain and drug withdrawal.

Missy slapped him again. "Answer me."

Louis muttered something unintelligible.

Missy's hand went to his throat and squeezed. Louis flushed bright red, veins popping out in his neck and face. Fuck.

"Missy—" Ben started.

"No," she said, never wavering, her sights locked on the man she was about to strangle. "He needs to say the words. Say it, Louis! You will never come near me again."

Louis was wheezing, his lips moving, no sound coming out.

"He's not worth it," Ben said gently, trying to reach his soft Missy. "Let's just get him out of here, okay? He got the message."

She looked down at Louis and finally released her hold. The man gasped for air.

Missy got off him. "Get out."

Louis scrambled to his feet, nearly tripping in his hurry to get out the door.

Missy slammed the door behind him, locked it, and put the chain on, breathing heavily.

Ben stared at the door for a moment, trying to understand how Missy could have been with someone like that. She deserved so much better.

He turned to her. "You married that piece of shit?"

Her eyes flashed, but her voice was deadly calm. "I never told you I was married. Who told you?"

He didn't respond right away, unsure how to answer without outing himself. On the other hand, he didn't want to lie.

She leveled accusing eyes on him. "Omigod, I'm so stupid. You looked me up on Checkin, didn't you? Invaded my privacy!"

He held up a palm. "Okay, let's just take a minute. You're worked up right now."

"Just tell me if you looked me up on Checkin without my consent."

"Missy, that was standard procedure."

"Go to hell!" She whirled, grabbed her coat and purse, and marched out the door.

He couldn't let her go out alone. What if Louis was lurking around the corner?

He shoved his feet into his boots and grabbed his jacket, his gut churning into full-out dread. He knew it had been too perfect. Nothing good ever lasted.

He followed her out the door anyway.

14

Missy raced downstairs, berating herself for ever trusting Ben. How many times did it take for her to really understand no man was trustworthy? The sick feeling in her gut told her she'd let herself be fooled again. Fooled by Louis, fooled by the married Matt, and now Ben. All of those women she'd counseled so they wouldn't be victims, all her years of being a victim had taught her, rightly so, never to trust a man. And she'd stupidly let Ben in close, to her home, her bed, her heart.

She dashed at the stinging tears in her eyes and scanned the parking lot for signs of Louis. In the distance his old blue Toyota sped out of the apartment complex. She was shaking, sweating, her entire nervous system crashing hard after the adrenaline rush of finally facing Louis after all these years and *fighting back*. She never would've confronted him. All of the self-defense she'd learned was only if someone struck out at her. He'd rushed at her, she'd defended.

She'd prevailed.

She took a deep breath, still too worked up to drive anywhere. She slipped into her car, turning it on and blasting the heat. She quickly locked the doors. She'd wait for Ben to leave, and then she'd go back inside. Why should she be the one to leave her own apartment? She'd fled the scene, not able to handle Ben's betrayal on top of seeing Louis. She'd nearly killed Louis, had felt that power in her hands, her vision a red haze. Ben's voice had reached through that haze, bringing her back to herself. She'd thank him for that if she wasn't so furious with him. He'd spied on her without her consent, learning personal information she never shared with anyone.

Ben appeared at the bottom of the stairs and immediately zoned in on her, striding toward her car. Dammit. She didn't want to talk to him. He'd seen way too much today, knew way too much. This was why she never had relationships. They always hurt her.

He knocked on the passenger's side window, gesturing for her to open the door.

She looked at him and all she saw was a man who knew more than anyone had a right to. She rubbed her temples. Why couldn't she ever leave the past behind and be a new person? A smarter, stronger Missy. Now it was too late. Ben would always see that other Missy—a victim.

"I'm freezing out here!" Ben shouted through the closed window. "Come on, Missy. Please unlock the door."

She glared at him.

"I'm not going away until I know you're okay!" he shouted.

All his noise was going to attract the attention of her neighbors. She gritted her teeth and unlocked the door.

He got in, shut the door, and turned to her, speaking in a rush. "I looked into you when you first started working for us. It's standard procedure for all employees. That's what we do."

She reached for calm, still shaky and sweating. "I didn't sign anything saying it was okay to look that deeply into my background. Checking references, yes. My personal history, no. And you ne-never—" She clamped her mouth shut, hating that she was stammering. Her throat was thick, tears welling in her eyes, but she would not break down.

"Can we go back inside to talk?" he asked gently. "Maybe give you some time to recover. I know Louis—"

"No-o!" Her breath hitched, a sob trying to break through that she ruthlessly pushed down. "You never told me that was standard procedure."

He stared at her for a long moment. "I'll admit I was driven by curiosity, and I didn't follow any of our standard procedure when it came to you. I was hooked, Missy. From the very beginning, I couldn't think straight when it came to you. There was never any bad intention, I swear. I just wanted to get to know you."

"Then you should've let it happen naturally over time. When I was ready."

"You're right. I see that now and I'm sorry."

She pursed her lips, fighting tears.

He let out a long breath. "If you would've just talked to me, I wouldn't have been so curious. You were so mysterious."

Her hackles rose. "So this is my fault?"

"Look, here's what we need to do. I'm going to apologize again, you're going to be mad for a while, and then everything will go back to normal. Okay? I'm really, really sorry. I won't ever do anything like that again."

She said nothing.

"I told you I never had a serious relationship. Can you cut me a little slack? I fucked up and I'm sorry."

Her lower lip wobbled. She had to end this. She couldn't trust him.

His tone became more forceful. "Missy, you should've told me about Louis. That he hurt you. You kept me in the dark about your life. Without all the information, I can't fix it."

She pressed her lips together. "I'm not something for you to fix."

"Not you, just the problem. That's who I am. I see problems and find solutions. Just give me all the information. You've barely shared anything about yourself. The only things I know are you grew up in California and love snow."

She crossed her arms, her chin jutting out. "You know a lot more than that, stuff I've never told anyone besides my sister."

"I still feel in the dark," he said quietly. "Like you're hiding something."

Fuck it. He wanted the grisly details, she'd give them to him. Maybe then he'd realize exactly how fucked up she was. She was sure he'd be sprinting out the door.

"What do you want to know, Ben? That my mom had me at sixteen and gave me up? How about the story of my adoptive parents dying in a car crash when I was ten? My dad dead on arrival, my mom in a coma, me looking at her full of tubes and wires, terrified, and then she died overnight while I was sleeping and I never got to say goodbye? That's a real winner. Or that I married that bastard Louis at eighteen and endured three years of abuse? That he held my wrists and slapped me so hard my ears rang, yanked my hair out, hurled emotional abuse at me, and I let him? How about that he nearly killed me when I mentioned divorce? Is that what you're so damn eager to find out?"

"Missy." He reached for her hand, but she resisted, keeping her arms crossed.

Her mouth kept going with no thought beyond driving him away. "Add this to your Missy file. I was a fifteen-year-old runaway after my aunt's sleazy husband made a pass at me. Six months on the streets, then a series of foster homes. Isn't it great how much you can learn about someone even without the magic of the internet?"

"No, Missy, I'm sorry. Baby—"

Tears choked her voice. "Fuck you."

His voice remained calm and steady. "I'm really sorry for what you've been through."

She stared straight ahead, tears flowing freely. "I didn't want you to know. He abused me and I stayed."

"That wasn't your fault."

She wiped her tears and sniffled. "I know, but it feels like it. I came here to start fresh. I didn't want you to see me like this." She crossed her arms again, hugging herself. "I'm so embarrassed," she whispered.

"Embarrassed? Hell, I'm impressed. You kicked his ass and he fucking deserved it."

She met his eyes, seeing only appreciation. "It felt good," she admitted. "I've been training for that confrontation ever since I left him."

"You did good, Missy. You really did."

She nodded, still feeling shaky but also a little proud.

"How long has he been begging you for money?"

"He showed up a few weeks ago. I thought after he stole the money from the church bazaar, I wouldn't see him again. That's why I was working a second job. I didn't want anyone to know I brought the devil to their door."

"Again, not your fault."

"It is." Without her, Louis never would've come around.

"No, not your fault," Ben insisted. "Tell me everything that's happened with him, and then I'll figure out a plan to permanently get him out of your life. And then we'll help out the Harpers together."

"That is *my job*. I don't need you to rescue me."

"I'm not. I'm helping."

"I've got this," she said evenly. She fixed her own problems. Always.

"Why won't you let me help?" he barked, his voice too loud in the confined space.

She glared at him. "Don't yell at me. I don't need or want your help."

He blew out a breath. "Look, I don't want to fight."

"Then you should go because I'm in no mood to get it through your thick head. I fix my own problems."

"You can't do everything by yourself," he snapped, sounding really pissed that she wasn't immediately falling in line with his fix-Missy plan. "I want to help. I want to keep you safe."

"I am safe. You say you're impressed with how I kicked ass, but you don't think I can handle any further confrontation. I can. I don't think there will be a next time with Louis, but if there is, I will be prepared."

"What does that mean?" he demanded.

She closed her eyes, trying to keep from screaming. She

didn't like answering to Ben. He wanted to take over, be her Mr. Fix-It, and that was just not her. "Ben, I'm done."

"Done?"

She met his eyes and spoke over the lump in her throat. "Yes."

"Okay, we can talk later, but don't think I'm letting it drop."

She shook her head.

Understanding dawned, his expression going slack. "Are we...breaking up?"

"Yes," she whispered and stepped out of the car, gently shutting the door behind her.

A moment later, the car door slammed behind him.

He didn't come after her.

She walked on shaking legs by sheer force of will, nausea rolling around her stomach, and made it into her apartment before collapsing.

15

———

Ben dragged himself into work on Monday morning, a mess of tangled emotions—angry, sad, and hurt all at the same time. It astounded him how much he hurt. One weekend of perfection and then it all fell apart. All along, he'd known the happiness he felt with Missy couldn't last, yet he'd been blindsided. It was like a severed limb. She'd felt like an essential part of his life and now she was gone. He still couldn't believe how quickly everything turned to shit.

Logan took one look at him and stopped pouring his coffee. "You look like hell. Pull an all-nighter?"

He'd probably managed three hours of sleep after turning the Missy problem over in his mind for hours. "I slept." He trudged to his office, guilt weighing him down. He should've told Missy he'd looked into her background. No, he should've had her sign the standard form they gave everyone, but he'd gotten ahead of himself, eager to know more about her.

He slumped at his desk. Was it really so bad what he did? Or was Missy extra sensitive because of that asshole Louis? If she'd only shared more about herself, he wouldn't have been so curious.

He leaned his elbows on his desk and covered his face with his hands.

A soft knock on the door had him jackknifing upright. Had Missy shown up? Was she willing to talk to him again?

Logan.

Ben scowled. "Go away. I've got a lot to wrap up before Christmas." The office would be closed starting tomorrow, Christmas Eve, through the New Year.

"Wrap up?" Logan grinned and took a seat in the chair across from Ben's desk. He never could take a hint. "What'd ya get me?"

"I'm not in the mood to talk. Just please leave."

Logan studied him. "You and Missy break up?"

"How did you know?"

Logan shook his head. "You're a moron."

"Thanks, idiot." He pinched the bridge of his nose and closed his eyes. "Would you please just leave me alone?"

"Nope," Logan said cheerfully.

Ben narrowed his eyes. "I really don't want to kick your ass. Not good for the business."

Logan snorted. "Like you could." They were pretty evenly matched and both knew it after years of wrestling each other and all of the guys. It was both sport and how they resolved problems. At least back when they were kids. Teenaged years had seen their share of bloody noses too. Now they were adults and liked to think they were past that. Though the way Ben was feeling right now…he wasn't so sure.

Logan shook his head. "Ya know, I cleared the way for your cranky ass, letting her go early so you could finally be with her, and then you fuck it up."

Ben stood, placed his palms on the desk and got in Logan's face. "Last chance," he growled in warning.

Logan slowly stood, forcing Ben to straighten so he wouldn't have to look up at him. "Whatever it was, just apologize."

"I did! Many times."

"Do it again. With flowers or some shit like that."

Missy wasn't the kind of woman easily swayed by an obvious token of apology like that. Her trust level was low as it was, and what little trust she'd had in him, he'd managed to shut down completely. His chest ached, sadness pushing out all the anger and hurt. He slumped back to his seat. This sucked so bad.

"Damn, Ben, just looking at you is making me tear up."

"Fuck you."

"If she's that important to you, don't give up. It's not as hopeless as it feels right now." Logan turned and left.

"What do you know?" Ben shouted after him. Logan hadn't given up on his college girlfriend, still holding out hope for a reconciliation when "the time was right," whatever that meant. Ben didn't see that ever working out for Logan. The man knew nothing about fixing relationships.

Logan shot him the bird over his shoulder.

Ben clicked over to his email inbox, figuring at least he could clear that out. He certainly couldn't focus on any real work.

Delete. Delete. Delete.

Missy at the church bazaar, selling him a sweater, all smart-mouthed fun. That mouth, those sexy plump lips.

Delete. Delete. Delete.

Missy in a clingy black dress at the *Fierce Loving* wrap party, casually asking if he wanted to get laid. "An itch you need to scratch once in a while, right?" His finger hovered over the delete key, remembering the warm inviting look in her brown eyes. He'd thought the casual-sex thing was perfect, but then it turned into something more, and now it was *over*.

Delete! Delete! Delete!

He slammed the laptop closed, memories of Missy flashing through his brain—elf Missy, naked and primal Missy, buttoned-up professional Missy, soft Missy. He missed that Missy most of all, soft and tender. Undone by him.

He straightened. Wait a minute. That was all he needed to do. Some gesture that made her come undone, that showed her how much he loved her. His mind boggled for a moment. He did love her. Why else would he feel like he'd lost a part of himself when he'd lost her? He'd do something to show her she could trust him to come through. She'd understand she didn't have to deal with every fucking thing in life on her own. He helped the people he was close to. It was an essential part of him. She had to understand he helped because he loved.

He stood, pulling his jacket on, determined to get through to Missy. He stopped. What was he going to do, show up at her apartment? No. The Harper family. Missy would be going there tomorrow for Christmas Eve. She wanted to bring the Harpers a special Christmas celebration, and he'd help too, showing Missy they could be a great team if she'd just let him in. He pulled out his phone, searching for their address, but it wasn't listed anywhere. No problem. He knew they went to the same church as his grandmother. He'd get the info from her. He fired off a quick text to Logan, saying he'd be back in a couple of hours. He headed out the door, hope giving him an extra burst of energy.

By the time he got back to the office, it was hours later because he'd gotten hung up at his grandmother's house. She'd insisted on feeding him lunch and also gave him the third degree, asking if he was taking good care of himself, eating right, exercising, getting enough sleep, blah, blah, blah. He did his best to reassure her, but she seemed to know something was off with him. In any case, she'd been very helpful about the Harpers. After hearing their situation, he understood exactly why Missy was taking their cause so personally.

He just hoped his gesture didn't blow up in his face. With Missy, sometimes good intentions weren't enough. She had to believe deep down that he meant it.

16

Christmas Eve started out terrible and went downhill from there. First thing in the morning Missy discovered the Christmas turkey she'd planned to cook for the Harper family was rotten—tinged gray and reeking. Then the supermarket was sold out of turkeys. The whole meal had been planned around the turkey, so she'd driven to two more supermarkets, finally finding one the right size, but it was frozen solid. She'd settled for two roast chickens. Then she'd slipped on a patch of ice in the supermarket parking lot, landing mostly on her hip. It hurt like a sonuva bitch, and she was sure she'd have a massive bruise.

On the way home she got caught in crawling traffic near the Eastman mall, cursing all the last-minute shoppers to hell.

And now that she was finally pulling into the parking lot of her apartment building, the thin hold on her composure blew right along with her tire.

She swore a blue streak, smacking the steering wheel several times before pulling into a parking space, the car shaking and clunking along. To say that her Christmas spirit was low was an understatement. She felt like Scrooge, wanting the whole thing to be over with. Though she knew it wasn't just the stupid turkey or traffic or her flat tire, she was miserable over Ben. She missed him and hated that she missed him. Hated that her bed felt empty, hated that she saw his teasing blue eyes and ready dimpled smile every time she closed her eyes, hated that she felt so much for a man she couldn't trust. She knew the high cost of love, yet she'd stupidly let him into her heart. He wasn't as awful as Louis, she knew that, but he'd still hurt her. And she wouldn't let him hurt her again, even if she was miserable for a while. It would pass. She was a survivor.

She left the tire for later, grabbed the grocery bag, and went up to her apartment to get started on the cooking. By noon she was feeling a little calmer, or maybe she was just tired. She'd gotten up at five a.m. to get started on the meal preparation. The chickens were cooked; all the side dishes were prepared and in plastic containers. She'd made home-made apple pie last night. Now she just had to change the flat tire, load the food, decorations, and gifts into her car, and drive to the Harpers' apartment. She'd already confirmed with Rena that she'd be home this afternoon for a quick visit.

Missy changed her tire with the spare in the trunk, pleased with her competency. She used to have to call triple A for help, but her brother-in-law, Nico, had been happy to show her and Lily some basic car-maintenance skills. She admired her handiwork for a moment. The tire was smaller than the others, but it should hold for the ten-minute drive across town. She slowly stood, her hip sore from squatting on the ground to change the tire. She shivered in the damp and cold and looked to the sky—a pearly gray that promised snow. Oh, how she'd love to have a white Christmas. But not yet. She still had a lot to do for Christmas Eve.

She made her way back upstairs to her second-floor apartment, sore but determined. Three trips later, her car was packed to the gills with the perfect Harper family Christmas. She blew out a breath. Okay, she was back on schedule. It was time to bring the merry.

"Merry, merry, merry," she chanted, willing herself to cheer up as she slowly pulled out of the lot, the car rocking with the low spare tire.

Only two traffic lights to get through, slowly and steadily

she made her way through town, then turned onto Main Street. So far so good. She turned right at the church, the Harpers' apartment wasn't far now, three blocks down, one over. *Bam!* Her heart raced at the sound and she gripped the steering wheel tight as the car lurched to the right. She'd hit a pothole she hadn't seen. What the hell, she could barely steer. She slowly pulled over to the curb, the car shaking violently. This could not be good. She got out and stared at the culprit— her spare tire had a flat. Grrr…

She looked up and down the street at the rows of houses all decorated for Christmas, the families inside probably enjoying their pre-holiday preparations. She wouldn't disturb them for help. She could do this. All she had to do was walk four blocks with her stuff. Sure, it might take a few trips, but she'd get it done. First decorations, she'd leave those on the front porch of the Victorian where the Harpers rented the third-floor attic apartment. Hopefully none of the kids would notice her until she was all set. Then presents, then the food.

She delivered the decorations—two boxes in her arms plus two bags slung over her shoulders. Her hip was sore and her face felt frozen, but whatever.

Next the presents. She wrestled the garbage bag full of gifts out of the backseat, then retrieved the wrapped picture frame with a gift certificate for a family photo session from the trunk. She couldn't chance that breaking. She was about to set out when a man called out to her.

"Need any help there?"

She turned to find the owner of the house she was parked in front of, an elderly man with balding white hair, peering at her from his front porch, where he stood in a flannel shirt, loose slacks, and slippers. "No, thanks," she called. "I've got it."

He approached, checking out her car. "Looks like you got a flat."

"Yes, I'll deal with that when I get back."

He rubbed his hands together and blew on them. "You got another tire?"

"No. It's okay. I'll get a tow and walk home."

He gave her a sympathetic look. "How far are you walking? I could give you a ride." He smiled. "A young lady shouldn't be walking far on a cold day like today."

She took a step away, uneasy with his offer. "It's not far, thanks. I'll be out of your hair quick as I can." She took off and didn't look back. The bag of gifts bumped her hip painfully and she had to switch it to her other side. She soldiered on, ignoring her sore hip, frozen face, numb fingers and toes. One more trip.

Thankfully, by the time she returned to her car, the older man had gone back into his house. This trip would be a little tougher. Four bags of food and the pie wrapped in aluminum foil. Luckily she'd used her sturdy handled grocery bags. She arranged two bags per shoulder and carried the pie. Oh, she almost forgot. She'd bought two homemade jars of jelly from the craft bazaar. She snagged that plastic bag, hooking it around her wrist. She felt a little like a packhorse, shoulders aching, hip protesting, but she carried on.

Almost there, you got this, ignore the pain, ignore the cold.

She reached the front path to the Harpers' home and looked up as she walked, the lights were on in their apartment. It made her smile thinking of the joy on the kids' faces when they saw all this Christmas cheer—

"Ah!" She tripped on the uneven sidewalk. The pie flew from her hands, the jars of jelly slipped out of the bag to the sidewalk with a crash, and she fell sideways on top of the food bags, no doubt squishing the homemade cheese popovers. She shifted off the bags and just sat there on the cold sidewalk, surveying the broken glass, the ruined pie, and the goopy red and blue jelly splattered everywhere. The kids would've loved that strawberry and blueberry jelly, their favorites, for their peanut butter and jelly sandwiches. It was the little things that made kids feel secure. Her throat tightened. She'd wanted that so much for them.

She lifted her head to the sky, fighting back tears. This day had been hell and she suddenly wished she had some help. None of this would've happened if she'd only called Lexi or Sabrina for a ride. They lived just down the hall. Or she could've called Lily or Nico, who lived in town, to help with all of the bags. At the very least she could've borrowed someone's car. She'd done it all herself, just like always, and now she was cold, tired, sore and about to have the mother of all breakdowns. Everything hurt, everything sucked, everything was just too damn hard.

A hot tear leaked out and she wiped it away. No. She was stronger than that. This was a delay not a failure. She just needed to empty a bag to get rid of the glass safely, then she'd clean up the mess, and they'd still have their Christmas dinner. The kids needed to know that even without their dad in the picture, even in a new place with very little money, they could still enjoy Christmas. How she wished she'd had someone to make that happen for her as a kid after her parents died. Her aunt couldn't have cared less about Missy's Christmas or anything else for that matter. She got to work, reorganizing the bags, and then carefully picked up the broken glass and put it in the empty bag.

She walked back to the house where her car was parked, put the bag of broken glass in the trunk of her car, and then knocked on the door of the older man who'd tried to be helpful earlier.

He answered the door with a smile. "I thought you'd be back with this weather. Thirty degrees gets into your bones. You want a ride home now?"

"No, thanks. I was hoping for a roll of paper towels and a garbage bag. I dropped some jars of jelly and a pie a few blocks away."

He gave her a strange look but told her he'd get them.

Time was ticking away as she rushed back to the Harpers' place. She was sure any minute someone would notice all the bags and boxes she'd left on the porch and front walk. She got there just as a young woman was peering down at the pie and jelly mess.

"That's mine," Missy called. "Sorry, I'll clean up and clear this out. I'm on my way to visit a friend upstairs."

The woman nodded and went back inside.

She squatted on the sidewalk, cleaning up as best she

could. She'd take a hose to it later after the festivities. Her hip was screaming in pain, but it had to be done. It just wouldn't do to leave a mess out here. Finally she was done, wiping her hands as best she could before gathering the decorations and buzzing Rena's apartment.

"Hi, it's Missy."

"Come on up."

She balanced the boxes on her non-injured hip while she opened the door and made her way up to the third floor. She knocked and the door swung open a moment later to a beaming Rena. Her dark brown hair was short now in a cute pixie cut. She wore a red sweater with jeans, looking comfortable and happy.

"Merry Christmas!" Missy exclaimed. "I brought some decorations. I wasn't sure if you'd brought much with you." Everyone knew they'd left with only one bag each of personal belongings.

"Oh, how nice. Here, let me help you with that." Rena took one of the boxes before Missy could protest.

She walked in to a cozy scene, a fire crackling in the fireplace, the scent of pine and fresh-baked cookies in the air. They had a scraggly Christmas tree in the corner decorated with candy canes, red and green construction paper chains, and silver tinsel. The kids were gathered around the coffee table, industriously cutting folded white paper into snowflakes.

"Hi, guys," she said. "That looks fun."

The boys ran over, showing off their snowflakes. "Aren't they awesome?" Todd asked. "We're going to put them on the tree next."

Will chimed in. "You can get really tricky, cutting in just the right place to make a surprise hole in the middle."

"Cool," she said.

Madelyn smiled, shaking her head. "It's not a surprise after the first time."

A timer dinged in the galley kitchen. Rena smiled. "Oh, that's our snickerdoodles. Just be a minute."

Missy left the decorations by the tree, thinking she'd probably brought too many. The tree was pretty well covered already, and they had snowflakes to add too.

She followed Rena to the kitchen, where the sight and smell of snickerdoodles made her stomach growl. A pang of pure longing went through her at this beautiful scene of family togetherness. "You really brought the Christmas cheer, Rena."

Rena took her potholders off and leaned close, speaking under her breath, "I wasn't sure how our first Christmas on our own would go, but the kids are happier than ever. They feel safe here. And they're resilient, you know? Their world was rocked and they carried on." She looked lovingly over at her children. "I never had time to do this kind of thing with them before, simple things like teaching them to make paper snowflakes. I was always so busy with all the kids' activities. I was more like a chauffeur and we barely had time to sit down to a meal together. Now we can't afford all those extras, but you know what? It taught us how to be a family again."

Missy couldn't speak for a moment, her throat tight, eyes burning with tears, heart pounding.

"Mom, help!" Will hollered, holding up his snowflake.

Rena walked over, and Missy just stared at the simple beauty of a mom helping her son make a snowflake. Rena's words stuck in her mind: *Their world was rocked and they carried on.* Missy's world had been rocked many, many times and she'd carried on too. She'd fought so hard and struggled so much, and she never gave herself credit for that. She was resilient. If her world was rocked again, she could carry on too.

She let out a breath, the ache in her heart easing. She could take a chance on Ben. He'd screwed up, but she had too, kissing him at the office, and he'd let it go. He'd apologized sincerely, there were no more secrets between them, and he might be willing to try again. She ran a shaking hand through her hair, both euphoric and terrified at the idea. What if it was too late?

Rena looked over. "Would you like to join us, Missy? Or I

could make you some tea and you could just relax on the sofa."

Crap. She'd left all the food and presents outside. "I'll be right back," she said. "I left something downstairs."

She raced out the door, hurrying down the stairs, hoping everything was still where she'd left it. She burst through the front door. Oh, thank goodness. She went for the bags of food first when a familiar masculine voice said in a wry tone, "Looks like a paintball war. I'd say red won." He meant the jelly stains on the sidewalk.

Heart in her throat, she lifted her gaze to find Ben standing at the end of the front walk in a green velvet coat with a matching green velvet elf hat, holding a brown paper bag. He was here because of her, she knew it, and that meant he hadn't given up on her. Her pulse raced, heat stealing through her body despite the cold, all of her suddenly electrically alive.

His dimples appeared and her heart squeezed. "I thought we could make sugar cookies. I brought the cookie cutters I used as a kid and sprinkles."

She slowly set the bags down and closed the distance between them on shaky legs. "How did you know where to find me?"

"My grandmother knows the Harpers. I wanted to help." He got serious. "I wanted you."

Words deserted her. She was trembling, hot tears stinging her eyes. He set his bag down and pulled her in for a hug, surrounding her with radiant love. Her body calmed as she snuggled into his warmth.

She looked up at him. "I forgive you. I want to try again, okay?"

"Thank God." He cupped her jaw, leaned down and kissed her. "Yes, yes, and yes."

A sound like someone tapping on glass reached them. Ben looked up and smiled. "We have an audience."

The kids were pressed against the glass, pointing at Ben and exclaiming excitedly.

"You do make a jolly elf," Missy said.

"I learned from the best," he teased. "This should be our Christmas tradition. Elfing on Christmas Eve."

"Elfing, huh? Sounds dirty."

He chuckled, pulled an elf hat from his back pocket and placed it on her head. "Perfect," he proclaimed. He looked around at the bags and the stuff on the porch. "Is all this stuff yours?"

"Yeah, I'll get it." She gathered all the bags of food. "It's for the Harpers." She straightened to find Ben already holding the huge bag of presents. "You don't have to carry that."

"I've got one measly bag of cookie stuff. Let me carry it."

She frowned and picked up the wrapped frame still in its plastic bag on the porch.

He closed the distance between them. "What's with the frowning? What're all these muscles for if not to carry stuff?"

She stared at him. "You understand I don't need that? It might take me two trips, but I can get it all upstairs by myself."

He searched her eyes for a moment. "Are you saying I can relax and let you take care of everything by yourself?"

She nodded, beaming. He got it now.

He leaned in and kissed her. "Do you know how long it's been since I could relax with a woman?"

"I have no idea."

"Never. I have never relaxed with a woman." He spoke louder in a bold announcement. "I swear as Santa is my witness I will never do anything to make you regret taking a chance on me again. Transparency in all things. Do you believe me?"

She melted, warm and gooey with all she felt for him. "I do."

Their gazes locked, an electric current zinging between them, the unspoken acknowledgment of her "I do" sounding like a marriage vow. It didn't scare her at all, and Ben looked happy about it too.

He smiled his sexy dimpled smile, his eyes shining with love. "I liked the sound of that, Missy. Now let's go upstairs.

We've got a Christmas Eve to celebrate." He jerked his chin for her to go ahead, still holding the giant bag of presents.

It would be easier to do it all in one trip with his help. Her practical side had her forging ahead with the food, feeling like they were a Christmas team. Elves got things done.

They reached the door and knocked. The door swung open and the boys exclaimed, "It's Santa's helpers!"

She and Ben exchanged a grin and walked in, a real elfing team.

17

Ben was just finishing up the Lego plane set with Todd and Will when Missy walked back in the door of the Harpers' apartment, her nose and cheeks bright pink from the outdoors, where she'd been hosing off the front sidewalk for the Harpers. She'd refused to let him do the chore, and he was still getting used to the idea of not taking over every job that needed to be done. It was a relief, actually, to know she could pull her weight and then some. And she'd forgiven his misstep. He couldn't have asked for a better Christmas present, his entire world righting itself again.

Madelyn ran up to Missy, excitedly showing her the beaded friendship bracelet she'd made for her new friend Katrina.

He swallowed over the lump in his throat. Watching Missy with the kids—all the thought and care she'd put into making their Christmas special—had been a revelation. She might've been through hell and back, but she was capable of great love and compassion. It wasn't just that she'd prepared a delicious dinner knowing Rena was still teaching herself to cook after years of depending on takeout. Or that Missy refused to take credit for the decorations and gifts, saying they were from the Clover Park community and she was just the messenger. The thing was, Missy made the practical gifts of winter clothing that some would've seen as charity sound really cool. She'd carefully selected jackets, snow pants, boots, hats, and gloves for the kids, wrapped them up, and declared them not just great for cold days, but also perfect for sledding, snowball fights, and making snowmen. Where most kids would've balked at clothes for a present, she got the boys excited about what they could do with them, and Madelyn was thrilled to have a coat very much like her friend Katrina's coat. He was sure Missy had looked into girl fashion ahead of time too.

After the clothes, Missy had given each kid a toy to open now and four more under the tree for Christmas morning. The boys got Lego sets, a plane and truck respectively, and Madelyn got a friendship bracelet maker. Missy had really gotten into making a friendship bracelet with Madelyn, talking to her the whole time, gently probing if she'd met some nice girls at her new school.

He watched Missy now, head bent, still standing in her coat, talking to Madelyn, and it hit him with a jolt—she was his first and last love. His pulse thrummed, all of his nerve endings tingling, alert and alive. He'd never let himself fall before, always one foot out the door, but maybe that was how it was meant to be so fate could bring Missy into his life. He wanted to spend the rest of his life with her, and he wanted to start right away. Marriage wasn't out of the question, though if Missy didn't want to get married again, he'd be just as happy as long as they were together.

He stood and went to help her off with her coat when Rena joined them, handing him the bag with his cookie stuff and his jacket.

"I washed the cookie cutters for you," Rena said. "You two have done so much. I can't thank you enough. I'm going to get the kids settled in for bed, try anyway—" she laughed "—so why don't you go ahead and enjoy your Christmas Eve together."

"Thanks so much for letting us celebrate with you," Missy

said. "Anything else you need, just give me a call. I remember what it was like to be new in town. I've got tons of connections for whatever you might need."

Rena shook her head, smiling. "I sure landed in the right town. I've never felt so welcome. And to think I found it so randomly. It was the only town with an apartment big enough for us that I could afford."

"Fate works in mysterious ways," Ben said, nudging Missy.

"I guess it does," Rena said softly. She turned to the kids. "Ben and Missy are leaving. What do you say?"

"Bye!" "Thank you!" "Merry Christmas!" the kids hollered in a cacophony of noise.

"You too," Ben said.

"Merry Christmas!" Missy called to the kids. She hugged Rena goodbye before heading out the door.

"Okay if I get a ride with you?" Missy asked on the way downstairs.

"Sure. My place okay? I'd like to spend Christmas Eve with you." And Christmas Day and New Year's Day and every day.

Her eyes went soft. "That sounds good."

He stopped walking to give her a quick kiss. Soft Missy got him every time.

They went downstairs and he held open the front door.

"I need to get my car towed," she said as she passed him.

Alarm flashed through him. Had she been in an accident? "Why? What happened?"

"Flat tire and then my spare tire got a flat. It's four blocks away."

They got into his car out front while he turned over this new information in his mind. Missy must've hauled all that stuff to the Harpers' apartment herself. He was sure she wouldn't have asked for help. He turned on the car, about to ask her how many trips she'd had to make for all that stuff when she shared all on her own, telling him this incredible story of one disaster after another that ultimately led to her goal of a happy Harper Christmas, though she confessed, they were already happy when she got there.

He stared at her, incredulous. "And at no point did it occur to you to ask for help? Not with the flat tire? Not with carrying so many things after hurting your hip? Not with the mess of broken glass, jelly, and pie?"

"It sounds ridiculous when you say it all like that."

"It *is* ridiculous. Even if you didn't want to call me, you've got friends and family in town."

"I'm just not used to asking for help." She bit her plump lower lip. "After the jelly jars shattered and the pie was ruined, I had a—" she heaved a sigh "—a brief moment where it occurred to me I probably should've asked for help."

He bit back a smile at her reluctant confession. "Well, you made it work." He put the car in gear and pulled into the street. "You made those kids really happy."

"I did."

"You're kind of like your own superheroine."

"I guess I am." She beamed and squeezed his arm. "And with your superhero complex, always wanting to rush to the rescue and fix everything, that makes us a good team."

He narrowed his eyes. "I hear an insult hiding in there."

"No, really, it's good," she insisted. "We're both competent people who like to help others."

"But…" He waited for the insult part.

She smiled to soften the blow. "But maybe you could help a little less, and I could ask for help once in a while."

"Okay. So…you think I'm a superhero?"

"Sure, in a way."

He relaxed. "Finally, she gets it."

"Arrogant much?"

"Uh, yeah. It comes from knowing I'm right."

"Uh-huh. So you say."

He glanced over at her; a small smile played over her lips. "Don't tell me you still think I'm Mr. Wrong." She'd called him that back when he hadn't recognized her with her red hair dyed brown. A play on his name, Mr. Wright.

Her lashes fluttered down. "No," she said softly. "I don't think that anymore."

His chest puffed with pride. "Say it, woman."

"You're Mr. Wright," she droned good-naturedly.

"I'm your Mr. Right and I don't mean my last name."

She gave him one of her soft smiles. "Yes."

He spoke around the lump in his throat, his voice gruff. "Thank you."

She let out a soft sigh. "I'm going to call my brother-in-law about my car. One of his guys will pick it up and take care of it."

"So *that* guy you call for help."

She rolled her eyes. "He owns a garage." She gave him a playful jab. "Don't worry, I'll find something for Super Ben to do one day."

"Yeah, yeah."

"I will! Promise. How about tonight you rub my feet for me? That would be a real help."

"Okay, but, fair warning, my hands will wander."

She laughed. "I was counting on that."

She pulled out her phone and arranged for her car to be taken care of, then closed her eyes and fell asleep. He wasn't too surprised, it was dark out, the car was warm, and she'd been up since five working like a dog. He turned the volume up on the radio, singing along to "I'll be Home for Christmas" in a low sleep-friendly tone, thinking of how much he wanted to bring Missy with him for Christmas dinner at his grandmother's house. Christmas Eve would be just for them.

After he pulled into his garage, he turned off the car, considering carrying Missy to bed when she suddenly lurched upright. "Where am I?" she asked, sounding alarmed. "What time is it?"

"You're at my house," he said in a soothing tone. "It's close to nine."

She relaxed. "Oh. Sorry. Sometimes I startle awake if something feels off. A reflex from when I didn't feel safe from one day to the next."

"You're always safe with me."

She put a palm to his cheek, giving him soft Missy eyes, before getting out of the car. He followed behind, turning on lights and then heading for the family room to light a fire in the fireplace.

"You got a tree!" she exclaimed, rushing over to check it out.

He flicked the switch for the multicolored Christmas lights on the tree. "It's artificial, but yeah. Looks real enough." He always did the tree up, each ornament a reminder of his mom. She'd given him one every year for Christmas, usually related to food (the pizza ornament had been his favorite as a kid) or his favorite sports teams. He also had ornaments from their vacations and crafty ornaments he'd been forced to make at school. Some of his masterpieces—a pinecone with glued-on sequins, a toilet paper roll turned into a Christmas tree (sort of), and a plaster handprint from preschool. His mom had loved every crappy last one of them. Maybe one day he'd have his own kids' crap on the tree and think it was special.

He smiled to himself as he got the fire going, listening to Missy *ooh* and *aah* over the tree. After he finished with the fire, he retrieved the flat box he'd wrapped in the colorful Sunday comics for her weeks ago from under the tree. The comic wrapping paper was another Christmas tradition with his mom.

He held the gift out to her. "Here. Merry Christmas."

She clapped a hand over her mouth, her eyes wide.

He laughed. "Don't look so shocked. It's Christmas. Of course I got you something." He pulled her hand from her mouth and placed the box in her hands.

She stared at it, then at him. "Ben! I didn't get you anything." She stared at the box again, shaking her head. Then she gave him the soft eyes. "You're so wonderful. I was miserable without you."

He smiled big time.

Her lower lip stuck out. "You don't have to look so happy about it."

He took her by the elbow and walked with her to the sofa. "I'm glad you were miserable without me because I felt like I'd lost a limb."

She set the box on the coffee table and hugged him tight, burying her head against his chest.

He hugged her back, took a deep breath, and spoke in a rush. "Missy, the reason I was so mad when we kissed at work was because I couldn't risk looking unprofessional. I was falsely accused of sexual harassment by a woman I hired and fired."

Her head shot up.

"I was cleared of all charges. I was never even alone with her. I was sure another strike against me would destroy my career and ruin our chances with investors. I couldn't risk being seen as inappropriate with you. That's why Logan was taking the lead for those meetings. Word had leaked out about the sexual harassment charge."

"But you said it was cleared."

"I know, but it still looks bad even to be accused."

She scowled. "Anyone who knows you at all would know you'd never do anything like that! You're the best man I've ever met!"

A surge of love shot through him, his chest puffing out with pride. "Thank you."

She scowled some more. "It's true. I can't believe someone would do that to you."

He framed her face with his hands and gave her a quick kiss. "Even though I was being professional with you, every day I was building on our friendship, hoping when the time was right, it would be more."

Her eyes went soft and she leaned her cheek into his hand. "Oh, Ben. I-I love you."

His pulse skyrocketed, all of him charged and alive. He was about to say it back, but she kept talking straight from the heart, her eyes shiny with unshed tears. "I haven't said those words to a man since my ex-husband. I've been afraid to love. I thought it would make me weak, but with you I can still be strong. And safe."

He felt like dancing on the coffee table, pure elation surging through him. "That is the best gift I've ever been given."

"Really?" she asked uncertainly. She'd taken a risk on him, and he knew that was big for her.

He stroked her soft cheek with his thumb. "Really. I love you too. I've loved you since you tried to sell me a bird sweater—"

She laughed.

"And I will love you until the day I die."

"Ben," she choked out, swiping at her eyes, "don't say things like that. You make me cry."

"It's true." He guided her to sit on the sofa with him and set her present in her lap. "Come on, open your present."

She stared at the Sunday comics. "It's so cute. Do you always wrap with the comics?"

"Yeah. It was a tradition with my mom. I keep her traditions as a way to honor her memory. She always made holidays special." He swallowed hard. "Most of the holidays are reminders of her."

"That must be difficult for you."

He nodded. "It was at first. But now it's almost like she's with me."

She gave him a quick kiss before tearing the paper off and lifting the lid of the shirt box. "Oh!" She pulled out a red cashmere sweater. "It's gorgeous! Did you get me red because you miss my red hair? Because even if I went back to red, it would clash with this."

"I hadn't really thought about it. I just thought it would cling to your luscious breasts."

She kissed him and said in a teasing voice, "Now you're making me feel dirty."

"Excellent. More on that later."

She rubbed her cheek against the sweater, smiling.

"Would you like to have Christmas dinner with me at my grandmother's house?" he asked.

She put the sweater in her lap. "Oh. Usually I spend Christmas with Lily's family. Maybe I could do Christmas morning with them and Christmas dinner with you." She set the sweater on the coffee table, retrieved her phone from her purse, and joined him on the sofa, texting rapidly. A moment later, she held the phone up to show him.

Lily: *I knew he was Mr. Right!*

"So you told her about Mr. Wrong?" he asked, playing with a lock of her hair.

She set the phone on the table. "I was forced to after she kept bugging me to bring you to Sunday dinner. It's step one in a lasting relationship."

"Awesome, I'm there." He nuzzled her neck before whispering in her ear, "Now if you pass the grandmom test, you can move in with me."

She pulled back to look at him. "Oh, really? Only if I pass?"

He grinned. "Just mind your manners and I'm sure you'll pass."

She lifted her chin. "Maybe you have to pass a test too."

He gestured for her to bring it on, wiggling his fingers. "I'll ace it."

She stared at him, her eyes wide and searching. "Does it really not bother you knowing about my past?"

"Missy," he said gently, "I had a lot of the same experiences."

"Not Louis."

He took her hand. "No, but that would never change my opinion of you."

She stared at their joined hands. "Do you see me as a victim?"

His chest tightened in sympathy. "Is that how you see yourself?"

"I was back then," she said softly. "Which is why I didn't want you or anyone to know because then you'd see me that way. The only person who knows is my sister."

He squeezed her hand. "Anyone who knows you now would say victim is the furthest thing from who you really are. I look at you and I think *strong*." She smiled a little, so he kept talking. "Practical. Stubborn. Sexy as hell. Smart-mouthed. I can keep going."

"Please do," she said with a bright smile.

He gazed at her, his heart full. "I look at you and I see my forever love."

She threw herself on top of him, kissing him all over his face. He laughed and lay back, taking her with him, wrapping his arms around her and kissing her back in what quickly became a hot and heavy make-out session. Only one way this was going to go—rolling onto the floor with his sexy wrestling alligator woman. He was about to suggest they take it upstairs, where they'd have a softer landing with all her wrestling, when she lifted her head and smiled down at him.

"What?" he asked.

"Too bad you didn't buy that bluebird of happiness sweater. I'd love to see you wear it Christmas morning."

He cupped her ass and squeezed. "And I'd love to see you in nothing but your elf hat. Maybe some strategically placed jingle bells that I could ring."

"Pervert."

"You say that, but I can tell you're thinking about it. Your cheeks and neck are pink."

"That's from your stubble."

He rubbed his jaw. "I'll shave tomorrow."

"You're kind of a sweetie, aren't you?"

"How dare you." He sat up, taking her with him, and she grinned. He kissed her, then lifted her off him, setting her on her feet. "If anyone's a sweet thing, it's you all soft and naked in front of the fire." He took her hand and led her to the hearth.

When they got to the warmth of the fire, she threw her arms around his neck and spoke against his lips. "What if I'm not sweet? What if I'm, as you so romantically put it, in wrestling alligator form?"

He kissed her and lowered her to the rug. "That wasn't a complaint. I love your alligator. I'm happy as long as you're naked."

She wrapped her arms around him. "Make love to me."

His heart stuttered. Not fuck me, *love* me. His voice gruff with emotion, he cupped her face with both hands. "I will love you body and soul." His eyes stung, hers were glossy with tears, and they met halfway for a searing passionate kiss that held all the love in the world.

18

Missy followed Ben up the path to his grandmother's ranch home in Eastman, a little nervous to meet the woman who'd raised Ben after his mom's death. She needed to make a good impression because she knew his grandmother meant the world to him. His grandmother had moved into the house Ben had grown up in so he'd have that stability. Missy wished her aunt would've done the same. It wasn't easy to start over in a new home and new school while grieving her family.

They reached the concrete front porch, and Ben entwined his fingers with hers, gave her a quick kiss, and rang the bell. His easy affection was a nice distraction. One day she'd get used to it, she supposed, but now it gave her a small jolt of surprise every time.

The door swung open and Missy's jaw dropped. Sweet Mrs. Walsh from church stood there in a red sweater with a big Christmas tree on it that blinked with tiny multicolored lights. She had a small red bow clipped to her white jaw-length hair. Ben stepped inside, swallowing his petite grandmother up in a hug. Missy followed behind, her mind whirling.

His grandmother pulled away from Ben and beamed at Missy. "I knew you'd be together by Christmas!"

"I didn't know you were Ben's grandmother," Missy said,

looking at Ben and then back to his grandmother. Of course, there was no family resemblance since Ben was adopted. Their last names were different too, so she couldn't be faulted for not putting it together before.

"Proud to be," Mrs. Walsh said. "Come in, come in, have a seat. Merry Christmas!" She muttered to herself as she hustled into her living room, where a plate of peanut butter cookies waited. Each cookie had a Hershey's Kiss pressed in the center.

Missy took a seat next to Ben on the cushy beige sofa. Mrs. Walsh sat in a blue high-back chair next to them, looking delighted, a big smile on her face.

Ben took a cookie. "Thanks, Grandmom. Love your peanut butter Kiss cookies."

"That's why I made them," Mrs. Walsh said. "Always take care of my cutie patootie."

Missy bit back a laugh. Ben just grinned.

A bizarre thought occurred to Missy. "Mrs. Walsh?"

"Yes?" The older woman's blue eyes twinkled with glee.

"Did you send Ben to the church bazaar specifically to meet me?" Missy asked.

Mrs. Walsh laughed. "I sent him to get his gift."

Ben chuckled. "Which was Missy. I get it now." He made a face at his grandmother and asked in mock anger, "Now what made you think I wanted to be set up?"

"You're thirty-one years old, for crying out loud," Mrs. Walsh retorted. "Single and wilting on the vine. Besides, Missy here is like you, a good person with a deeply compassionate nature. Good people. Two good people who belong together." She smiled smugly.

Missy exchanged a wry look with Ben. They'd been had, a total setup, but both of them were too happy to care. Maybe they'd both wanted to believe in fate. You know what? Maybe some of it was fate. After all, it wasn't like Mrs. Walsh knew Missy, like Ben, had been adopted and lost her parents. She'd never shared that kind of personal info with anyone but her sister. There was something unique about her and Ben's common backgrounds that bordered on the mystical.

"Ha!" Mrs. Walsh exclaimed. "I'm not hearing any complaints. Of course, Ben here is slow to make his move—"

"I am not slow," he protested. Missy laughed.

Mrs. Walsh continued as if he hadn't spoken. "So I had to make a little more effort. Missy, when I saw you working as an elf at the mall, I sent him over the very next day for a watch battery. That watch has been dead for years!"

Missy grimaced. "I'm not sure seeing me as an elf actually helped my case. I looked utterly ridiculous."

"You looked adorable!" Mrs. Walsh declared.

"And the short skirt helped too," Ben put in with a wink.

Missy laughed and shook her finger at his grandmother. "You're tricky. I never would've guessed it was you behind all those times I ran into Ben. I thought it was just because he and I worked in the same town and knew a lot of the same people."

Mrs. Walsh held the plate of cookies out to Missy. "Eat. You're too skinny." The sweetness of the gesture made Missy's throat catch. Mrs. Walsh was looking after her like family.

Missy took a cookie. "Thank you."

Mrs. Walsh nodded once and declared, "I told Ben he'd marry a redhead." Everyone at church had seen Missy with red hair for a short time.

Ben groaned. "Subtle."

Missy took a bite of cookie, not commenting on the marriage thing. She knew Ben wasn't on board with marriage, he'd told her that before, and she wasn't too keen on the idea after her traumatic first marriage.

"See?" Ben said to Missy. "Fate is real." He gestured to his grandmother.

"I'm fate," Mrs. Walsh said with a cackle. "Admit it, Ben, isn't the gift of Missy better than that itchy sweater? I told you to get your gift before someone else snatched her up. She's quite a catch."

Missy's cheeks flushed, not used to compliments.

"Yes, she is," Ben said with a smile. He leaned close and

whispered in her ear, "Looks like you passed the grandmom test long ago."

"What're you whispering over there?" Mrs. Walsh demanded. "I can't hear you."

Missy smiled. "He says I passed the grandmom test."

"You did! I picked you!" Mrs. Walsh rubbed her hands together. "So when's the wedding? I'm not getting any younger, you know."

Missy choked on a laugh.

"We're going to shack up first," Ben said matter-of-factly.

Shack up? Missy turned to Ben, shaking her head that he'd talk to his grandmother like that. He gave her a wide-eyed look like *what?*

"Living in sin!" Mrs. Walsh declared with a scowl. Then Ben made it worse.

"Missy is the worst kind of sinner."

"Ben!" Missy exclaimed.

He nudged Missy's arm, looking at his grandmother. "She looks so angelic, but you should see her—ow!" Missy had elbowed him in the ribs.

Missy smiled sweetly at him. He gave her a kiss and nipped her lower lip in retaliation. A jolt of desire shot through her and she had to fight the urge for more.

"Who wants wine?" Mrs. Walsh asked. "I think we should toast to Ben finally settling down." She stood, muttering under her breath, "Even if it is living in sin." She headed into the kitchen.

Ben took Missy's hand, his voice low and husky. "I'd marry you in a heartbeat."

Missy sucked in air. "What're you saying?"

He lifted her hand, brushing his lips across her knuckles, raising tingling goose bumps up her arm. "If you were open to getting married again, I would love to marry you. You're my first love." He paused, gazing deep into her eyes. Heart thundering, she held his gaze. "My last love. I want to spend my life with you."

She burst into tears, overwhelmed with everything she felt for him, overwhelmed by his tender words.

He wrapped an arm around her shoulders and pulled her in close. "Too soon," he murmured. "We'll talk later."

Mrs. Walsh walked in a few moments later with the wine tucked under one arm, holding a corkscrew, three wineglasses clutched by the stems in her other hand. Missy quickly wiped away her tears, but his grandmother caught the movement.

"Benjamin Oliver Wright!" Mrs. Walsh bellowed. "What did you do?"

"Thanks for the vote of confidence," he muttered.

Missy straightened in her seat. "He just said the sweetest thing, and it made me cry because I'm not used to sweetness."

"Oh." Mrs. Walsh handed Ben the bottle of cabernet and the corkscrew. "Well, that's okay then. Ben can be sweet sometimes, though usually just with family. You're the first woman he's brought home."

Ben opened the wine and poured, not seeming the least embarrassed to have his grandmother sharing so openly about him. He handed Missy a glass of wine, and she gazed at him in wonder. She had no idea this was such a special occasion. She'd assumed he'd brought home many girlfriends over the years.

"Is that true?" Missy asked him. "I'm the first woman you've brought home?"

"Yup."

Her chin quivered, her eyes welling up because he was so special to her too. The only man that both excited her and made her feel safe.

He took her glass from her trembling fingers, setting it on the table. "If you cry again, Grandmom's going to blame me."

Missy grabbed both of his hands in a tight grip. "I will marry you."

He flashed a brilliant smile. "You will?"

She nodded, beaming at him. He cupped her face and kissed her passionately. And she returned that kiss with all the love in her heart.

"Enough sucking face," Mrs. Walsh finally declared, making them laugh.

They pulled apart, smiling at each other.

"Let's have that toast," Mrs. Walsh said, lifting her glass.

She and Ben picked up their glasses too, lifting them high.

"To me!" Mrs. Walsh exclaimed. "For bringing two wonderful people together who will soon make me a great-grandmother!"

Ben jolted. Missy just smiled and joined in the toast. She'd longed for children, but hadn't wanted to be a single mom. If she was marrying Ben, building a life with him, then she'd love to make kids part of that too.

"No rush on kids," Ben said, sending his grandmother a significant look. Mrs. Walsh smiled serenely.

Missy could just imagine his grandmother making inquiries into their reproductive life. *Have you been trying? What position did you use? Hurry up and try again!*

Ben gave Missy's hand a squeeze, giving her a small smile, his dimples etched in his clean-shaven cheeks. "Down the line, kids would be great with me."

Missy's throat clogged with emotion, her eyes hot. All she could manage was, "Me too."

"Now you're going to make me cry," Mrs. Walsh declared. "So much love." She sniffled. "I'm so happy. This old woman needs a hug."

Ben went and hugged her, and Missy followed quickly after him. They all settled into their seats again, and Missy told Mrs. Walsh about the Harpers' Christmas Eve celebration. They all talked for a good while, sipping wine, warm and toasty, everything aglow. Or maybe that was just Missy glowing from all the love.

Later, she and Ben went into the kitchen to help with dinner. Mrs. Walsh kept up a steady stream of Ben stories that ranged from ridiculously proud to downright embarrassing. Missy loved it, frequently checking in with Ben, who merely smiled, not seeming bothered that she now had the most thorough background check on him a person could have. Forget the internet, nothing like a grandmother to spill the good stuff. Her absolute favorite was his brush with fame at twelve years old in a boy band that toured local malls. Ha! She told him she couldn't wait to see those pictures and he definitely had to sing something for her. He promised he would, but he would exact payment for the privilege. Which they both knew was his version of dirty talk with a senior citizen witness.

Dinner was delicious and relaxed. She'd already gotten along with Mrs. Walsh before and felt even closer to her now over their shared love of Ben.

She gazed across the table at Ben as he bent his head to take a bite of spiced cherry pie. It was his grandmother's famous recipe. She quickly took a forkful herself, popped it in her mouth, and then nearly spewed it out when Mrs. Walsh exclaimed, "Ben, you've got to get her a ring! It's not official without the ring. Don't delay."

"I don't need a ring," Missy quickly said. "It's okay." She didn't need a lot to be happy. She'd learned to live with the basics.

Ben held up a palm, shooting his grandmother another significant look before telling Missy, "You're getting a ring and a formal proposal. I just wanted you to know right now how much I'd like to be married to you. You make me believe in marriage. I just..." He lifted one large shoulder. "I just want you forever."

Missy's breath caught at "forever," her heart clutching, her body frozen. And then she let out a shaky breath and, with no thought other than to be as close to him as possible, she moved as if in a dream, leaving her seat to walk around the table to him. He was standing when she reached him, and she just wrapped her arms around his middle and hugged him tight. His arms came around her, filling her with radiant love.

He dropped a kiss on top of her head and told his grandmother, "I'm taking her home now."

Missy pulled back and looked over at his grandmother, who was discreetly wiping tears away.

"Get out of here," Mrs. Walsh said, shooing them away. "Go make babies."

Ben chuckled. "Subtle, she is not."

"Subtle doesn't get the job done," Mrs. Walsh said. "*I* get the job done."

Missy couldn't fault Mrs. Walsh for taking credit. The woman had a vested interest in their relationship and got them talking about marriage and kids. Missy was sure she never would've broached the topic for a very long time. It was almost too much to hope for. She would've been content with a committed relationship, but had to admit that marriage and kids were a welcome addition.

They said their goodbyes and drove to his place, already making plans for her to move in. For the first time, thoughts of the future filled her with nothing but joy.

But the moment they stepped inside his house, Missy had enough talking. She pounced on him, and they went for it right up against the foyer wall.

And again in his bed.

And in the shower.

Then they fell asleep, a tangle of arms and legs, all resistance gone, surrendering to fate, surrendering to love.

Missy sat on Hailey's mushy floral sofa, along with Lexi and Sabrina, the three of them already dressed and ready for New Year's Eve. The rest of their friends were scattered around Hailey's apartment, poking through her stacks of bridal magazines and romance novels in the living room bookcases, in the kitchen enjoying some of the veggies and dip Hailey had put out for them, or in Hailey's bedroom putting the finishing touches on their hair and makeup under Hailey's enthusiastic direction. They'd all shown up here—as far as Hailey knew—for a group pre-New Year's Eve party prep. The party at Garner's had become their annual tradition. The real reason they were gathered at Hailey's apartment? Sabrina was holding an intervention.

When Hailey finally appeared in the living room—stunning as always in an off-the-shoulder black shirt with black miniskirt and black stilettos—Mad made an excuse to go, saying she'd forgotten something at home.

"What is it?" Hailey asked. "You can borrow something of mine."

"All good," Mad said, already heading to the door. "Won't be long."

Hailey's brows scrunched together. "She's going to be at

least half an hour by the time she drives to her place and back."

"No hurry," Sabrina soothed. "It's not even eight yet."

"I suppose," Hailey said, her brow creasing. "Anyone hungry?" she asked brightly, heading to the kitchen. "I'll make up a cheese and cracker platter. Ooh, I have some olives too."

Missy and Sabrina exchanged a look. It was Sabrina's professional opinion, which they all agreed with, that Hailey needed to calm the frick down. She'd been running on hyper speed for more than two months, ever since Josh and Clarissa got together, and Sabrina feared Hailey was going to burn out. It was a real concern because Hailey's wedding planning business would require a lot of work in the first half of the new year, not just from newly engaged couples, but also from Carrie and Zach's wedding, which would be featured in the national magazine *Bride Special*. That wedding had to be the wedding to top all weddings. For Hailey's mental health and the future of her business, this intervention was a must.

They could hear Hailey chattering a mile a minute to sweet Lauren, the only one who'd stayed behind in the kitchen when the Hailey whirlwind arrived. The rest of them chatted quietly in the living room, waiting for the signal from Mad. Half an hour later, appetizers consumed and all of them on the edge of their seats, Sabrina announced, "Mad's on her way." That meant Mad was here, waiting just outside.

"Finally!" Hailey called from the kitchen, where she was finishing the dishes. She'd refused to let anyone help, saying she enjoyed keeping busy. "We've got to dance tonight, ladies! I'm so antsy being stuck indoors in the winter." Antsy, hyper, same deal.

"Sounds good to me," Lexi called.

"Hailey, could you come in here?" Sabrina asked. "I wanted to talk to you about the new year."

"Just a minute!" Hailey caroled. "Let me just…" Some dishes banged into cabinets and then Hailey appeared in the living room. "Okay! What're you planning?"

Missy shifted to the arm of the sofa and Sabrina patted the

empty spot next to her. Hailey headed over and sat, crossing her legs, and turned to Sabrina. "What can I help you with?"

The room quieted. Everyone prepared to take Sabrina's lead. She was the counselor, after all.

Sabrina spoke in a gentle tone, her words direct. "Hailey, now that the holidays are over, it's time for you to slow down."

"You've been scary hyper," Missy put in.

Hailey huffed. "I'm not scary hyper. I've just been—"

"Working hard," Sabrina interrupted. "Ever since—" she paused and Missy held her breath, wondering if Sabrina would confront Hailey on Josh "—well, ever since you decided to be open to relationships, ending your friends-with-benefits situation, you've had lots of loving energy pouring out."

"All over the place," Lexi said.

Sabrina sent Lexi a quelling look before turning back to Hailey. "And we all think you need to…focus that energy. It's your turn to be loved." She texted Mad for the signal while the rest of them chimed in with all of their good intentions.

"She's right!"

"You deserve love!"

"We want you to be happy!"

Hailey gulped, her eyes shifting around the room nervously.

There was a knock at the door. Hailey jerked upright, stiff as a board, staring at the door like the devil himself might walk through, Josh being the devil.

"I'll get it," Sabrina said, rushing to the door and opening it.

Mad stepped inside carrying two duffel bags. "I'm back!"

Hailey sagged on the sofa. "Gah! I thought you ladies were doing some matchmaking, reversing the tables here."

"We totally should've done that!" Lexi exclaimed. They all shot her a dark look. "What? Turnabout is fair play."

Mad carefully set the duffel bags on the floor, opened one and pulled out a little scrap of white wiry-haired dog with too-big pointy ears and huge black eyes. The dog looked around curiously. Rose was a one-year-old terrier-Chihuahua mix, a little homely with her spare wiry tufts of fur, but they'd all thought Hailey would enjoy prettying her up with lots of grooming and doggy accessories. The dog was small enough for an apartment, feisty like Hailey, and already trained from her previous owner, an elderly woman who'd died unexpectedly.

"You got a dog?" Hailey exclaimed. "Cool!"

Mad didn't reply, instead carrying Rose over to Hailey. "We thought a dog would calm you down."

"For me?" Hailey whispered.

Sabrina piped up. "Dogs offer unconditional love, and that's what we want for you. If you don't want the responsibility—"

"Are you kidding?" Hailey took Rose from Mad's arms and cuddled her against her chest. "I love him already." She got nose to nose with the dog, who licked her mouth. "He kissed me!"

"It's a her," Missy said. "Her name is Rose, but you could change it."

"It's perfect." Hailey stroked the dog behind the ears. "Aren't you so precious?" Tears leaked out of Hailey's eyes, which Rose promptly licked. Sabrina stood, rubbing Hailey's back, and smiled at the little dog. If Hailey hadn't wanted Rose, Mad had planned to keep her. Or Sabrina. They both thought she was great.

Hailey gave them all a watery smile. "These are happy tears. I'm just so touched that you thought of such a wonderful present for me." She laughed and cooed to the dog. "Yes, you are a wonderful present! Who's a cutie? You are!" She cuddled Rose against her, and the dog reached her front paws up to Hailey's bare shoulder and rested her head between them. "She's like a furry baby!"

"Wire-hair dogs are supposed to be more hypoallergenic," Sabrina said, "so you might be able to take her to work with you. Your clients should be okay."

Hailey stroked Rose's little head. "Of course I'm bringing her to work! I'll get her a little doggie bed and she can stay in

my office. That's one of the perks of owning my own business. In fact, she's such a tiny thing, I'll bring her everywhere.
I'll get one of those purses for dogs."

Mad held up the duffel bag with mesh sides. "This is her
carrier."

"Great! I'll put her in that with the top open and take her to
the party tonight. It's a good idea for her to get used to lots of
people. After all, she'll probably be attending a lot of weddings."

"Uh, sure," Mad said uncertainly, looking to Sabrina.

"You should probably check in with each client before you
do that," Sabrina said. "And give it a little time to see how
Rose will feel about that."

"She's fine!" Hailey declared. "Look, here she is with all of
us and she's so calm. She's nearly asleep on my shoulder."
She turned to show them Rose, who was indeed resting, eyes
droopy, on Hailey's shoulder. Probably a pretty warm spot.
"Thanks again, ladies, this is the best gift I've ever gotten."

"She's pretty good," Mad said. "She's been at my place for
the last couple of weeks. She's housebroken and knows how
to sit, beg, and lie down."

Hailey stroked Rose's tiny body. "She's smart. I can tell
already."

Mad retrieved the other duffel bag and put it on the
kitchen counter. "This is her food, bowls, leash, and treats."

"Thanks, Mad," Hailey said, her voice choked. "Thanks all
of you. Group hug."

They all gathered close, hugging Hailey and petting little
Rose, who didn't bother to open her eyes. She'd found her
safe spot with Hailey.

After their hug, Hailey shifted Rose into her carrier,
zipped it up, and made more baby talk at her through the
mesh panel. She straightened. "I feel more relaxed already.
Who's ready to party?"

"Party!" Lexi shouted, which made Rose growl in
warning.

"It's okay, baby," Hailey cooed to Rose. "Mama's here."
She pulled on her white wool coat. "I'm driving over so Rose

doesn't get a chill. I've got room for two more if you want a ride."

They all piled into the available cars and drove the short distance to Garner's. Hailey rented a basement apartment in an old Victorian in Clover Park only a few blocks away.

By the time she got to Garner's, Missy couldn't wait to tell Ben how great their doggy intervention had gone. He'd been skeptical, saying Hailey might not even like dogs. The bar was crowded, noisy with conversation and rockin' music from some speakers set up around the space. The tables had been cleared from the dining area on the right side to make room for more mingling. Along the half wall separating the dining area from the bar, a long table of appetizers had been set up. All the usual culprits—hot wings, pigs in blankets, and warm tortilla chips.

She went on tiptoe, trying to find Ben. She knew the guys were here somewhere, but the bar was open to the community, so there were tons of people here she didn't know too. She texted him, telling him she was here.

Hailey came up behind her and put a hand on her shoulder. "Can you hold Rose for a minute while I take off my coat? I don't want her to get accidentally stepped on."

"Sure," Missy said, putting the carrier strap over her shoulder. Rose was so light.

Hailey shrugged off her coat. White fur clung to her chest where Rose had been resting.

Missy gestured to Hailey's shirt. "You should probably get a lint brush."

Hailey glanced down at what was no doubt a designer shirt and picked some off with her fingers. "Guess I better get used to it." She took the carrier back and unzipped it. Rose sat up, looking all around, her nose twitching as she sniffed the air. "Come on, I think Rose would like one of those pigs in blankets."

"Sure." Missy followed her over there, checking for a text from Ben. *On my way.* That was weird. She'd thought for sure he'd be here by now.

They got to the table, and Hailey took Rose out of her carrier.

"What is that?" Josh asked, appearing suddenly, staring at Rose. He poured fresh tortilla chips into the warming bin.

Rose growled.

"What do you mean, what is that?" Hailey asked. "This is my dog, Rose. She's learning socialization."

Josh closed the distance between them. "You sure she's a dog? She looks like a rat."

Hailey gasped, indignant beyond words. Rose bared her tiny teeth at Josh, growling, making the little dog look even more homely.

"Not much of a looker," Josh said, reaching out to pet Rose. The dog barked and barked and barked. Ear-piercing, high-pitched, teeth-jangling barks.

Hailey stepped back from Josh, staring at Rose, who finally quieted, then at Josh. "She doesn't like you."

Josh bared his teeth at Rose. "Maybe I don't like her."

Hailey stroked Rose, talking to her soothingly as she retrieved a pig in a blanket, feeding Rose a tiny piece.

"Those are for paying customers," Josh said.

"I'm paying," Hailey said.

"No dogs allowed," Josh said, crossing his arms.

Missy took a quick peek around for signs of Clarissa. If Josh and Hailey were going to get into it, Clarissa would surely intervene. She didn't see her.

"Is Clarissa here?" Missy asked Josh.

"No," he said, his eyes glued to Hailey's dog. "There are health codes, you know."

Both Hailey and Rose growled at Josh.

"Will Clarissa be here soon?" Missy asked Josh.

A muscle ticked in Josh's jaw, but he remained quiet, staring at Hailey.

"She's no trouble," Hailey insisted, wiping Rose's muzzle clean of flaky pastry crumbs from the pig in a blanket. "Are you, babykins? You just stay in your little carrier, happy as can be."

Josh stepped closer and Rose erupted in ferocious earsplitting barks.

Hailey stared at Rose and eased away from Josh. "My goodness, that is some bark." She looked to Josh. "You'd better go. She really doesn't like when you get close."

"This is my bar!" Josh snapped. "If anyone has to go, it's that little rat."

Hailey scowled. "It is not your bar. You just manage it."

Josh clenched his jaw, glaring at Hailey before stalking off.

Missy watched him go, hoping Clarissa would be here soon because Missy had never seen Josh in such a foul mood. Josh retreated behind the bar and went back to work, filling drink orders.

"Maybe you should take Rose home," Missy told Hailey. "Josh said no dogs allowed. It is a restaurant."

Hailey lifted her chin. "Rose is my therapy dog. You're allowed to have therapy dogs in restaurants."

"How can she be your therapy dog when you just got her? Don't you have to have special training for that?"

"We'll start our training right after the new year. In the meantime, she's my emotional therapy dog. I do feel more relaxed and calm when she's with me."

"But Josh—"

"Can pry her out of my cold dead hands." Her icy tone was surprisingly intimidating coming from the normally perky woman.

"Your call," Missy said. Her phone vibrated with a text from Ben. *I'm here. Meet me by the front door.* "Gotta go," she told Hailey, who didn't notice, she was so busy cooing to little Rose.

Her eyes locked on Ben standing in the entryway in his usual black leather jacket, faded jeans, and hiking boots. Her heart thumped a happy beat and she practically ran into his arms, hugging him. "Happy New Year!" she exclaimed.

He smiled, his eyes warm and tender. "Not yet. Soon."

"What took you so long?"

"I had a few things to do around the house."

She stared at him in confusion. "You were late for the party because you were cleaning?"

"You'll see," he said mysteriously.

They joined their friends, everyone in good spirits. Soon she was dancing crazy with her friends, Ben watching her with open amusement and affection, Missy's heart full to bursting with all the love and friendship in the room. The time just flew by.

Next thing she knew, it was nearly midnight, and Josh turned off the music for the big countdown.

"Almost time!" Hailey shouted. She handed Rose's carrier to Mad and stood on a chair, holding up ten fingers for the countdown. All eyes were on her—the women shocked that Hailey would climb up on a chair in a miniskirt. With her hands in the air, her midriff was exposed too. She was in great shape, all toned and curvy. The men stared at her bared belly while Hailey stared at the time on the TV over the bar with the Times Square New Year's Eve countdown.

Hailey started the countdown. "Ten…nine…eight—ah!"

Josh had appeared out of nowhere, lifting her by the waist off the chair. Rose barked ferociously at Josh, and Hailey took her dog from Mad, talking to her soothingly and quickly moving away from Josh.

Josh took Hailey's place on the chair, continuing the countdown, the volume in the room getting louder with excitement. "Five…four…three…two…one!"

"Happy…" Missy trailed off. The room was utterly silent. What happened? Why was everyone so quiet? She sucked in air. Ben was down on one knee in front of her, holding up a diamond ring.

"Missy Higgins, my first and last love, will you marry me?"

She slapped a hand over her mouth, trembling in shock. She nodded, her vision blurry from tears.

He smiled. "I need the words, sweetheart."

She dropped her hand. "Yes."

The room erupted in cheers. Ben slipped the ring on her finger, rose to his feet, and pulled her into his arms. She threw her arms around his neck and kissed him passionately. Wild applause rang through her ears, confetti raining down over them. By the time they came up for air, grinning like fools, their friends were busy wishing each other happy New Year.

All of the couples were kissing—Mad and Parker, Charlotte and Ty, Lauren and Alex, Carrie and Zach, Ally and Ethan. Sabrina accepted a kiss on the cheek from Marcus, as did Lexi. Logan elbowed Marcus out of the way and hugged Lexi. Logan then held out his arms to Sabrina, smiling and letting her come to him. Sabrina held out her arms awkwardly, all stiff, her arms at weird angles. They engaged in the world's most awkward hug—Sabrina patting his back with one hand, the other hand on his elbow—before breaking apart, both of them looking away. Weird. Missy had thought Sabrina, being a relationship counselor, would be much smoother with men. Well, she was a little shy. Maybe she didn't have a lot of personal experience. Sabrina had never shared much about men, but Missy had assumed that was because she was a private person.

"Let's get some champagne," Missy told Ben.

"A toast to a new year and a new life." He brushed his thumb over her lower lip and pressed on it before kissing her gently. "With my soon-to-be wife."

She beamed. "I love you so much I want to yell it to the world."

"Feel free."

"I love Ben Wright!" she shouted.

"We know!" her friends shouted back. Everyone laughed.

They headed to the bar, where Josh was already hard at work, pouring fresh glasses of champagne. They had a fantastic chaotic toast, everyone talking and laughing all at once before Hailey took control to properly toast to Missy and Ben. She was such an awesome friend.

Clarissa never did show up.

After a private toast with Ben that was more kissing than sipping champagne, she and Ben left, eager to go back to his place. Which would soon be her place too; Ben was moving her in tomorrow.

When they got there, he guided her into the house from the garage, one hand on the small of her back.

She stepped into the dark kitchen. "Turn on the light."

Ben put a hand over her eyes and turned on the light. "We're moving, we're moving," he said in her ear, guiding her through the house.

"What in the world are you up to?"

"You'll see." They moved quite a distance before he finally stopped. "This is why I was late." He dropped his hand from her eyes at the foot of the stairs. Rose petals were strewn on the stairs, making a path through the upstairs hallway. No one had ever made her a rose-petal path. It was so beautifully romantic. Her throat tightened.

"Ben," she whispered. That was it. She had no more words.

"I wanted our first night as an engaged couple to be special."

She turned to him with a smile. "You were pretty sure I'd say yes."

He kissed her and spoke against her lips. "We both know it was a done deal." He took her hand, entwining his fingers with hers, and walked upstairs with her. "You can't resist me. Besides our informal engagement in front of my grandmother is binding in a court of grandmom law."

She laughed. "I was not aware of that."

"Oh, yeah, serious stuff."

They reached the upstairs hallway and he gestured for her to go ahead. She followed the rose petals to the bedroom. The petals made a path to the bed, where he'd put more petals in the shape of a heart. He turned the light on, dimmed it, and then lit white candles set around the room.

She would've swooned if she were the type. As it was, she was overwhelmed by the generosity and tenderness of this man. She'd never experienced anything like it, and now she'd have the rest of her life with him. She was so damn lucky she could hardly believe it was all real. She watched him take off his hiking boots and set them to the side, still in a state of shock. How was this her life? The most amazing sexy loving thoughtful man in the world was her fiancé?

She blinked away tears, clearing her vision. He got in bed, lying sideways near the top of the heart and gesturing to it. "Climb on board, the love bed is ready."

She didn't know whether to laugh or burst into happy tears.

He let out a loud sigh, sat up and peeled off his shirt, revealing his bulky shoulders and sexy chest. "Fine. I'll up the ante. Get moving, woman."

She slowly walked over, feeling like she was in a romantic sexy dream. He stood and stripped off his jeans.

She leaped at him.

"There's my sexy alligator," he growled, and they rolled all over the soft petals, wrapped together in a hot tangle of love.

Dear Readers,

Hailey finally found unconditional love—with a dog. Who hates Josh. Will little Rose warm up to Josh? Will Hailey? Stay tuned. Logan Campbell and Sabrina might've had the world's most awkward hug on New Year's Eve, but their friendship is rock solid. Until it isn't. Next up is Logan and Sabrina's story, *Chance of Romance*, book 8 in the Happy Endings Book Club series. Join the club and get your happy ending!

Chance of Romance

When relationship counselor Sabrina Clarke gets a wedding invitation from the jerk who left her a jilted bride, she writes a scathing article on commitment-phobes that catapults her practice into the spotlight. But the publicity leads to unwelcome attention from a competitor who slams Sabrina for being single. *And, hello, stupid mistakes!* Sabrina panics in the middle of an interview and claims she's in a relationship with the friend she secretly lusts for—Logan Campbell.

Steamed is an understatement when Logan's long-distance relationship is derailed the moment Sabrina announces they're a couple on TV. Way to throw him under the bus! The pressure's on as Logan heads to California to repair his shaky relationship and navigate investor meetings for his tech company.

Sabrina knows she's got to undo the damage, but when she meets the rotten cheating apple of Logan's eye, she knows there's only one thing for her to do...make another stupid mistake.

Sign up for my newsletter and never miss a new release! kyliegilmore.com/newsletter

ALSO BY KYLIE GILMORE

Unleashed Romance <<steamy romcoms with dogs!

Fetching (Book 1)

Dashing (Book 2)

Sporting (Book 3)

Toying (Book 4)

Blazing (Book 5)

Chasing (Book 6)

Daring (Book 7)

Leading (Book 8)

Racing (Book 9)

Loving (Book 10)

The Clover Park Series <<brothers who put family first!

The Opposite of Wild (Book 1)

Daisy Does It All (Book 2)

Bad Taste in Men (Book 3)

Kissing Santa (Book 4)

Restless Harmony (Book 5)

Not My Romeo (Book 6)

Rev Me Up (Book 7)

An Ambitious Engagement (Book 8)

Clutch Player (Book 9)

A Tempting Friendship (Book 10)

Clover Park Bride: Nico and Lily's Wedding

A Valentine's Day Gift (Book 11)

Maggie Meets Her Match (Book 12)

The Clover Park STUDS series <<hawt geeks who unleash into studs!

Almost Over It (Book 1)

Almost Married (Book 2)

Almost Fate (Book 3)

Almost in Love (Book 4)

Almost Romance (Book 5)

Almost Hitched (Book 6)

Happy Endings Book Club Series <<the Campbell family and a romance book club collide!

Hidden Hollywood (Book 1)

Inviting Trouble (Book 2)

So Revealing (Book 3)

Formal Arrangement (Book 4)

Bad Boy Done Wrong (Book 5)

Mess With Me (Book 6)

Resisting Fate (Book 7)

Chance of Romance (Book 8)

Wicked Flirt (Book 9)

An Inconvenient Plan (Book 10)

A Happy Endings Wedding (Book 11)

The Rourkes Series <<swoonworthy princes and kickass princesses!

Royal Catch (Book 1)

Royal Hottie (Book 2)

Royal Darling (Book 3)

Royal Charmer (Book 4)

Royal Player (Book 5)

Royal Shark (Book 6)

Rogue Prince (Book 7)

Rogue Gentleman (Book 8)

Rogue Rascal (Book 9)

Rogue Angel (Book 10)

Rogue Devil (Book 11)

Rogue Beast (Book 12)

**Check out my website for the most up-to-date list of my books:
kyliegilmore.com/books**

ABOUT THE AUTHOR

Kylie Gilmore is the *USA Today* bestselling author of the Unleashed Romance series, the Rourkes series, the Happy Endings Book Club series, the Clover Park series, and the Clover Park STUDS series. She writes humorous romance that makes you laugh, cry, and reach for a cold glass of water.

Kylie lives in New York with her family, two cats, and a nutso dog. When she's not writing, reading hot romance, or dutifully taking notes at writing conferences, you can find her flexing her muscles all the way to the high cabinet for her secret chocolate stash.

Sign up for Kylie's Newsletter and get a FREE book! kyliegilmore.com/newsletter

For text alerts on Kylie's new releases, text KYLIE to the number (888) 707-3025. (US only)

For more fun stuff check out Kylie's website https://www.kyliegilmore.com.

Thanks for reading *Resisting Fate*. I hope you enjoyed it. Would you like to know about new releases? You can sign up for my new release email list at kyliegilmore.com/newsletter. I promise not to clog your inbox! Only new release info, sales, and some fun giveaways.

I love to hear from readers! You can find me at:
kyliegilmore.com
Instagram.com/kyliegilmore
Facebook.com/KylieGilmoreToo
Twitter @KylieGilmoreToo

If you liked Ben and Missy's story, please leave a review on your favorite retailer's website or Goodreads. Thank you.

www.ingramcontent.com/pod-product-compliance
Lightning Source LLC
Chambersburg PA
CBHW071258190726
48292CB00007B/2593